BYLINES & BLUE LINES

STEPHANIE JULIAN

MOONLIT NIGHT PUBLISHING

ONE

"You look as happy to be here as I feel. Can I buy you a drink?"

As a pickup line, Brody Mitchell knew it wasn't his best. Wasn't his worst, either.

Either way, he didn't give a shit right now.

He'd been the perfect son all fucking night.

He'd shaken hands with too many damn people to count, said all the right things and hadn't stuck his foot in his mouth once. At least, that he knew. He'd smiled until his face fucking hurt.

And he'd stayed until the very bitter end, even though he'd wanted to walk out fifteen minutes after he'd arrived.

Now, he was going to spend the rest of the night doing exactly whatever the hell he wanted.

And that included picking up a woman for sweaty, anonymous sex. Or at least making the attempt.

He'd made his way downstairs to the Haven Hotel bar, directly below the ballroom where his parents and sister continued to glad-hand blowhards with money and a hard-on for athletes.

He'd ordered a double Forty Creek, took a look around, and scoped out the hottest woman in the room.

Who turned to look at him like he was something she'd wiped off her shoe.

Par for the course today.

She didn't even bother to smile. "I'm meeting someone. Excuse me."

Then she hustled away, perfect hair swinging down the open back of her slinky dress almost to her mostly flat ass. She stopped to talk to another woman sitting at a table on the other side of the bar, who looked over the blonde's shoulder at him, then they both bolted for the exit.

"Well, shit."

Sighing in disgust, mainly at himself, he knocked back the rest of his drink and signaled the bartender for another. He wasn't driving tonight and he didn't have anywhere to be tomorrow until noon. He could get as shit-faced as he wanted and fuck himself into oblivion as long as he could get it up. Which would be for-fucking-ever if he drank the right amount of alcohol.

He needed to blow off steam, and sex was his release of choice. He just needed a willing partner. Sure, he could've found one upstairs. Several women had made it clear they'd be perfectly willing to spend the night in his bed. But those women wanted something from him he wasn't sure he wanted to give.

Puck bunnies were puck bunnies, no matter if they wore jeans and hockey sweaters or designer dresses. They looked at him and saw a notch on their scorecard. Or, worse, the ultimate prize—a pro-athlete husband.

He barely contained a shudder at the thought. He'd been burned before. Was in *no* hurry to repeat that debacle.

Tonight, he just wanted to lose himself in a woman who didn't know who he was and wouldn't give a fuck if she did.

Absently twisting his Calder Cup ring around his right ring finger, he stared out at the crowd in the bar. He'd just come back from two weeks in Bermuda with several of his Reading Redtails teammates. They'd won the American Hockey League championships in June and had decided to keep the party going. He was tanned and fit, thanks to being back at training for the upcoming season, and if he kept his mouth from running—

Beside him, he heard a muted huff of feminine laughter and turned to check out his neighbor.

First thing he noticed was her hair. Probably because it covered her face, but also because it was kind of unruly. Long and curly and mostly dark brown, but it had a little blonde and red in it, too. Pretty.

Nothing like the sleek, straight, perfect hair of the women upstairs. He wondered if they all got together at the beginning of the season and decided what style they were going to wear. It kinda freaked him out, honestly.

This woman clearly hadn't gotten the memo.

Point in her favor.

Next point in her favor...the beer mug on the bar in front of her.

The women upstairs wouldn't be caught dead with anything less than a glass of expensive wine or champagne in their hands. Wine gave him a headache.

Now, if she were drinking whiskey, he'd get down on one knee right now and propose.

No, you wouldn't.

True. Still, didn't hurt to check out his options. And since she was his only option at the moment...

He let his gaze travel from her head to her feet, propped on the rung at the bottom of the stool. She didn't look dressed for picking up men. Her shoes didn't have pointy heels that could pass as dangerous weapons, and her navy dress looked like something she'd wear to work. She looked out of place.

Kind of how he felt.

"Glad to know I gave you a laugh tonight."

Turning her head, the woman smiled at him. And Brody had the immediate sense that this was the woman he'd been meant to meet tonight, stupid as that sounded. Not one of those overly primped, too-much-makeup blonde Barbies upstairs.

Shifting on his stool to face her fully, he let himself look, because, while not in the same league as the woman who'd just left like her ass was on fire, this woman was...pretty.

No, wait. That didn't really do her justice, either.

She was...

"Sorry." She shrugged, one shoulder only. "Didn't mean to eavesdrop. Although you weren't really trying to be quiet, were you?"

She didn't look sorry, but she was right. It wasn't her fault she'd overheard him strike out.

"Didn't really feel the need to be, no."

Her expression held wry amusement and her eyes... Well, her eyes were gorgeous. Kinda green, kinda blue, a little brown. And wide, almost too wide for her face. Her full lips balanced them out and the rest of her face was all cheekbones and pointed chin surrounded by that hair.

He had to stop himself from reaching for a strand and winding it around his fingers.

Dude, you're being weird. Knock it off.

"So," she drew the word out to about five syllables, "you gonna offer to buy me a drink, too? Or do I have to be blonde and wearing a dress that costs more than I make in a month?"

He didn't bother to hide his smile as he raised his glass in a salute. "I'll buy you a drink if you promise to sit here and keep me company while I finish mine."

She gave him a look. And it wasn't flirtatious. At all. "Is 'keep me company' code for 'I buy you a drink, you owe me sex'?"

Now he laughed out loud, startled to find he was able to, considering his mood.

"Nope. Not at all. But I hope you'll sit here and share it with me. I could use the company."

Her eyes narrowed slightly. "Why's that?"

He gave himself a second to think about his answer. "Because I think...I'd rather be talking to someone than sitting here alone."

Before he'd left his condo tonight, all he'd wanted to do was make an appearance at his dad's welcome party then get the hell out. Tonight had been a formality in his dad's transition into his new position with the Philadelphia Colonials, and he'd wanted Brody there, along with his mom and sister and golden first-born, James Robert.

If their dad had his way, RJ would be in Philadelphia permanently.

And that was something Brody absolutely did *not* want to think about right now.

"Bad night?"

The woman's expression softened, her smile commiserating.

His libido sat up, took notice. Okay, maybe "keep me company" *was* code for sex.

"Nah, just... Hell, I don't even know what to say about my night, honestly. What about you? What are you doing here alone?"

Her eyebrows rose. "Who says I'm alone?"

That look and that tone probably made lesser men take a step back. Another point in her favor.

"Well, you're kinda sitting here drinking by yourself so..."

A little head tilt as she shrugged that lone shoulder again.

"Honestly, I don't really know what I'm doing here. Looking for something I'm not gonna find, apparently." Sighing heavily, she propped an elbow on the bar and rested her head on her hand. "So, yes, I will take that drink."

He motioned to her mug. "Another beer?"

She glanced at his glass. "What are you drinking?"

"Whiskey."

A quick nod. "I'll have one of those. Neat."

His lips curved in a smile. "A woman after my own heart."

She gave him another one of those looks—a little haughty, a little uninterested. "My daddy never dilutes his whiskey. Says it a crime against humanity. I never go against my daddy."

"Sounds like a smart man."

Nodding solemnly, she lifted her glass and drained the last of the beer in one ladylike swallow. "Extremely. Taught me many things."

"Why does it sound like there's more to the story?"

Her brows arched over those pretty eyes again and Brody felt his blood heat in his veins.

"There's always more to every story, isn't there?"

He raised his glass and swallowed the last of his diluted drink. "Amen.

Signaling the bartender, he ordered two double 40 Creek whiskeys, neat. Juan Pablo nodded and grabbed the bottle from beneath the bar. The owner of this hotel imported this special reserve straight from the maker. Specifically because Brody asked for it.

Jared Golden and Brody had very little in common, but what they shared made up for everything they didn't.

When his drinking partner looked at the bottle then back at him with a question in her eyes, he shrugged.

"Spent some time in Ontario. Got a taste for this."

"I've never had it before. Not sure I've ever heard of it."

Picking up his glass, he tapped hers then took a swallow.

"Let me know what you think."

She sipped at the liquid, lips pressed against the glass in a way that really shouldn't make his gut clench and his cock respond the way it did.

His gaze slid down to her throat to watch as she swallowed, then back up as she ran her tongue along her bottom lip to catch a lingering drop.

Lust already a dull rush in his blood, it now became a roar. Maybe he wouldn't end up alone tonight after all.

"Mmm, this is amazing." Her smile widened and his lust blazed deep in his gut. "Why have I never heard of this?"

"Probably because it's not widely available in the States. Glad you like it."

"Thank you. I may have to make a trip to Ontario just for this."

"You should."

"I probably will be for work, actually."

It was on the tip of his tongue to ask what she did for a living, but that would inevitably lead to questions about what he did.

And honestly, he didn't want to be a professional hockey player and all the shit that went with it tonight.

He'd played the part for the last three hours, and now, he wanted to chill with someone who didn't treat him a certain way because of what he was and whose son he happened to be.

"Why were you in Canada?"

Does this woman really not know who I am?

The question flashed through his mind, but he dismissed it almost immediately.

Get over your damn self.

He didn't look like his roster shot tonight, not at all like the scruffy hockey player most people knew during the season.

He'd had a haircut yesterday, his usual unruly waves shorn down to almost nothing. His mother and sister had oohed and ahhed over how good he looked. He'd rolled his eyes and tried to brush them off. But his mom and Gabby ignored him, like always, and made a fuss. Hazards of being the youngest.

Since he'd shaved only an hour before he'd arrived, his jaw was still mostly bare of his typical dark stubble, though he felt the shadow starting.

He wore his glasses because his contacts had mysteriously disappeared somewhere between Reading and Philadelphia and he hadn't had time to search for them yet. And he was dressed in a suit. The suit wasn't unusual. He wore one every game day, but in the off-season, he only wore the damn thing when he had to make an appearance that demanded it.

Since he wasn't one of the Colonials' top-tier players, he didn't make a lot of appearances. At least, not the kind that required him to wear something other than a team-logo polo shirt and a pair of pants other than jeans.

But, thanks to his dad, all that was about to change.

And boy, is that gonna suck.

Tonight was proof.

"For work," he said, finally answering her question.

"Oh." She said that like she hadn't been expecting that answer. "Do you travel a lot for work?"

"Yeah." And he needed to shut down this line of questioning. "So, do you come here often?"

Her teasing smile told him she was going to let him get away with his dodge. It also made his dick hard.

"Not really, no." She waved her free hand around in the air. "Not my kind of place."

"Oh? What is your kind of place?"

She turned to look over her shoulder before looking into his eyes again. Another jolt of desire hit him low in his gut.

"Someplace a little less silk and a lot less money."

Nodding, he raised his glass in a toast. "I like the sound of that."

Her brows rose in mocking disbelief. "You look pretty comfortable here in your fancy suit."

Starting at his collar, her gaze boldly ran down his body, stopping at various points along the way—his chest, his waist, his thighs.

When her eyes rose level with his again, she had half a grin on her lips and a smile in her eyes.

Ask her. Just do it.

Just say, "Do you wanna get out of here?"

Would she leave with him? Would she say yes to a drink somewhere else? Like his apartment not too far from here?

Too soon? Probably.

Did he care? Not really. He really wanted to get laid. And she was checking every one of his boxes right now.

Sexy. Bold. Unintimidated. And she didn't seem to know who he was.

"I don't look half as good as you do."

Her eyebrows rose farther and her grin spread. "Thank you for the compliment, but I'm not," she waved a hand up and down her body, "exactly dressed for this place."

His turn to check her out openly, since she'd basically invited him to. He lingered longer than she had. Even sitting on a bar stool, he could tell she was short. Like, maybe five-three, at the most. She'd barely come up to his chin.

Typically, he went after tall, thin blondes. There were just so damn many of them. It was like an all-you-can-eat buffet in his world.

Why did women think athletes only wanted to date blondes?

Maybe because that's all you date.

Mentally shrugging off that thought, he went back to checking out his drinking partner. She wore a dress that probably covered her knees when she was standing but now exposed a couple inches of thigh. From what he could see, she had great legs.

Shit, he was staring at her thighs. His mother had taught him better manners than that.

His gaze shot back to hers and found her staring at him with a look that definitely expressed her thoughts. And he wasn't gaining points.

Still, she had to know how good she looked. He was just appreciating the sight.

So he gave her his most charming smile, which was pretty pitiful, truth be told. Most women thought he was an asshole. He didn't talk much and, when he did, made it clear he didn't do small talk. Just not worth the effort.

And flirting? Why bother? At the events he attended, all the women knew who he was. He didn't have to look hard to find a bed partner. Hell, he didn't even have to try hard.

She raised her eyebrows even farther. And that made him like her even more.

"From where I'm sitting, you're dressed...fine."

Her burst of laughter made his blood run hot. "They don't let you out much, do they?"

He couldn't help himself. He grinned. "Not a lot. But I've had all my shots. I'm safe."

She took another sip before answering. "Yeah, I'm not so sure about that."

"And I don't bite. Unless—"

Shit. God damn his mouth. Maybe she was right. Maybe he shouldn't be allowed out alone to hit on unsuspecting women.

Her smile widened. "Unless what?"

He shook his head. "I think I'm gonna keep the rest of that stupid statement to myself."

"And here I thought you were a man who speaks his mind."

"I'd rather be the man who knows when to keep his mouth shut. Although I have been told to use my words more often."

"Not a talker, huh?"

"Not really, no."

"And yet, here you are, talking to me."

True. And having no trouble finding words. Maybe not the right words but still...

"So how did I get so lucky?" she asked.

He wondered if she was being facetious. She didn't sound like it, but he'd never been good at reading women.

"Maybe you're just easy to talk to."

She closed her eyes for a second, made a little face, and nodded. "I might have heard that before."

"From your boyfriend?"

No one would ever accuse him of being smooth.

She stared straight into his eyes. "Don't have one of those."

Good to know. Unless... "Girlfriend?"

Gaze still steady. "I've got one or two of those."

He really liked her. "Any who'd be angry that we're sharing a drink?"

Her nose crinkled. "Most of my girlfriends think I need to get out more."

"I hear that from my friends, too. They tell me I need more socialization."

They could have a point.

She paused before turning to face him fully. Draping one arm on the bar and holding her glass with the other, she sat up a little straighter, leaned a little more toward him. Made him want to lean a little closer as well.

Now he could study her features more closely. And see

just how unusual they were. Exotic, even. Those beautiful eyes, wide lips, fine cheekbones, tilted-up nose. Dark-gold skin.

She became better-looking the longer he stared. And he was staring.

So intently that her lips curved again and those wide eyes narrowed down to slits.

"Yeah, sorry." He shook his head. "My friends say I'm feral."

She shrugged, shifting the v-neck of her dress just enough that he could see a hint of the upper curve of her breast.

Fuck.

"I'm used to feral," she said. "I grew up with three brothers."

Trying not to make it obvious that he was shifting on his stool to relieve his growing erection, he leaned an elbow on the bar.

"Oh yeah? Older or younger?"

"Two older, one younger. And two sisters. Both older."

"Wow. Your parents are either saints or crazy."

As soon as he said that, he realized that was absolutely the wrong thing to say about anyone's parents. And especially the parents of a woman he'd just met.

"Uh, wait, I didn't mean—"

"Crazy fits." She leaned back a little, lifted her glass and took another sip. "Definitely not saints. And they'd be the first to admit that. Even if they did adopt four of us."

"Wow. That's—" He didn't know how to finish his sentence.

She did it for him. "A lot of kids to handle. Yeah, it was chaos sometimes. But it was a hell of a lot better than foster care."

Yeah, he guessed it would be. "How long were you in foster care?"

"From the time I was five until I was nine."

"That must've sucked."

She shrugged. "Sure. Some days. What about you? Brothers? Sisters?"

And clearly she didn't want to talk about it. He might be feral but he wasn't stupid. "One of each. Same for parents. And they still hold hands after more than thirty years of marriage."

Her smile made his cock throb, which felt kind of weird considering they were talking about parents.

"That's so sweet. Mine do, too."

Yeah, to a girl, it probably was sweet. To him, it was just... whatever. They were his parents.

"So you never told me what you're doing here." She beat him to the punch to fill the silence that had started to string out. "Wait." She held up her hand and he kept his mouth closed. "Let me guess." She lifted one index finger to her lips and tapped them a few times. "You're an incognito bodyguard."

"Then I'd be a pretty shitty one because all my attention has been on you for the past fifteen minutes."

Her smile got a little sweeter. "Okay, you're here for the dog show."

"Hey, I just got my hair cut. I thought I looked pretty good."

It was the stupidest damn thing to say but she actually giggled. And his cock pressed even harder against his zipper.

What would she say if he asked her back to his condo? He was being uncharacteristically restrained, if he had to say so himself. If any of his teammates on either the Colonials or the Redtails could see him now, they'd be stunned. Right before they started making an ass out of him.

"You do look very nice," she agreed. "Are you here for a wedding?"

He shook his head

She took a sip of her drink. "Three strikes. I guess I'm out."

Since she really didn't seem to want an answer, he didn't give her one. And clumsily changed the subject.

"You follow the Phillies? Looks like they might make it all the way this year."

And there was that smile again. The one that kept his ass in the chair when he should've been long gone. He'd only intended to stop long enough for a drink and to pick up a woman before he headed home.

All his friends were hockey players and they were scattered around the world, visiting family before they returned to start conditioning, before their entire focus once again became hockey in September when training camp opened.

He had no wingman here to make sure he didn't act like an idiot. Had to make the dreaded small talk. But with her, it didn't seem hard.

For the next half hour, they talked baseball. She turned out to be more knowledgeable about the game than he ever would be, even though he'd played in high school. At least, he had for one season. Right before he'd made the decision for hockey to become his life.

The conversation shifted from baseball to football in a natural progression. And again, she was freakishly knowledgeable about the NFL. Hell, it almost seemed like she was dumbing down the conversation for him.

An offhand comment about a local musician led to a discussion about the local music scene but they circled back around to baseball.

But after a few more minutes, she shook her head. "Sorry about that. As you can probably tell, baseball is a bit of a religion with me."

"Have you always been a fan?"

She nodded, curls falling over her shoulders. "Oh yeah. When I was younger, it was a way for me to spend time with my dad. He'd take us all to the ballpark at least five or six times during the season, when he wasn't working. Now I know he took us because my mom needed a day off from six kids. But back then, I wanted to make the man who'd become my dad happy. Me liking baseball made him happy." She shrugged. "I mean, my brothers were into it, but my sisters were more interested in which player was the cutest. They'd sit at the end of the row and gossip about boys and whatever. They were already teenagers when I came along so I didn't really get where they were coming from. But my dad loves the game. He'd sit me on his lap and explain it while we watched."

"Sounds like you have a great relationship with him."

Her smile brightened as she nodded. "We do. I mean, I love my mom, but my dad and I share more interests."

"Do you get along with your sisters?"

"Yeah, but... I think they were expecting to get this pretty little princess to dress up and do my hair when Mom and Dad adopted us. So when I turned out to be the kid who would rather play football and baseball and who hated bows and jewelry, they weren't sure what to do with me."

"So you were a tomboy."

"Pretty much. Still am."

Again, it was on the tip of his tongue to ask what she did for a living. But he bit it back. Right here, right now, this felt good. Safe. Kind of like a moment out of time where nothing mattered and there were no consequences.

"So what about you?" She leaned her arm on the bar as she spoke. "Do you get along with your brother?"

And just like that, they were into unsafe territory. But she'd answered his questions. It was only fair he gave her a little bit of himself.

"Yeah, we do. Mostly. He's on the other side of the country so we don't really get to see each other much."

Except for the games they played against each other. And then there were the questions from the media, and he and RJ telling everyone how they enjoyed the rivalry, but in the end, they were brothers and family would always come first. Blah, blah, blah.

Brody knew RJ meant every word. And Brody did, as well. He just... *Shit.*

He was sick of all that shit. He just wanted to play the damn game.

Her gaze narrowed and he could tell she wanted to ask him more. He'd seen that look in the eyes of reporter after reporter, and he dreaded it every time. He didn't like to be interrogated. Or interviewed. Whatever. Same theory.

But here, talking to her, didn't feel like an interrogation.

"What about your sister? You get along with her?"

His grin came naturally. "Yes. She can be a total pain in my ass, but I love her."

"Is she older or younger?"

"Older."

"So you're the baby?"

"Yep."

"And are you spoiled?"

He opened his mouth to deny it then thought about his answer.

"Maybe a little."

"Do you always get what you want?"

Unconsciously, he rolled his shoulder, thought about the months he'd spent with the Redtails supposedly in rehab. He'd enjoyed the hell out of his stay in Reading. Most people figured he'd hate being down in the AHL. He'd loved it. He'd wanted to stay, which was something he'd told no one.

"Not always, no."

Her expression said she didn't really believe him.

Smiling, he leaned back and crossed his arms over his chest. "What? You don't believe me?"

"You look like the kind of guy who always gets what he wants."

"And that's a bad thing?"

He was genuinely curious to hear what she'd say. He watched her carefully as she stared back at him, her expression not giving anything away now.

He wondered what she'd look like when he had her spread out under him as he pushed inside her.

All that dark hair spread out on a pillow, her body naked and sweaty and pressed against his.

Shit.

He swallowed hard, trying not to let his thoughts how on his face. He didn't want to be that guy. The asshole who looked at a woman only as a sex partner.

And now you're being a hypocrite.

But this woman made him think about sex in a way he hadn't for months. Not just as a release but as a participation sport. Not that there'd been much release lately that didn't come from his hand.

"Not always, no," she parroted his words back to him. "Not if you're kind enough to give back to others as well as take what you're given."

Now, he generally wasn't a guy who paid much attention to banter. By the time he'd been a teenager and was supposed to be learning this girl-boy shit in high school, he'd been immersed in hockey. Before-school practice. After-school practice. Tournaments on the weekends. Development camp in the summer. Then the three years between sixteen and nineteen he'd spent in the OHL billeted with family friends. If he wasn't in school, he was on the ice or on a bus to a game.

He didn't see much need for banter. If you were honest about what you wanted, women either appreciated it or they didn't. If they didn't, he walked away. No harm, no foul.

It was on the tip of his tongue to ask if she wanted to go back to his condo with him and have sex. Wondered if he should at least know her name first, but then figured why ruin the fantasy.

She hadn't asked for his. Maybe she'd rather not know.

"So if I offer to make you come at least twice before I do, would that be good or bad?"

Yeah, his friends called him feral for good reason.

And maybe it was too much, too soon.

He watched as her eyebrows rose slowly and waited for her to huff in disgust and walk away.

It'd happened before. A few women came right out and called him a dick before they stalked off. Others left without a word. And then there were the ones who didn't actually give a shit how he talked and just wanted to fuck him because of who he was.

His problem, he realized a split second too late, was that he *did* care if this woman walked away.

Probably should've kept his damn mouth shut. He opened it to apologize for being an asshole—

"I guess," she said, "it would depend on how good you are in bed."

It took a split second for his brain to understand what she'd said.

But he definitely understood the look she gave him, even though they weren't squared off on a face-off dot.

Challenge.

He fucking loved a challenge. Never backed away when anyone threw one down in front of him. More often than not, he went out of his way to look for one. And not just on the ice. It was either just the way he was wired or it'd been ingrained in him from birth. You didn't grow up with a two-time Stanley Cup winner for a father and just decide on a whim to play the same sport.

No, you fucking worked your ass off to prove you deserved to play the same sport. Even though your older brother was considered the one with all the talent. Even though he'd had to work twice as hard to achieve the same success.

Like he said, he fucking loved a challenge.

Which meant that when this woman stared at him with that look in her eyes, he damn well knew what to do about it.

He grinned back at her.

TWO

"So, is that a question?" His voice deepened at least an octave. "Because if it is, I want to make sure I give the right answer."

Tara Downey watched the guy's lips curve into a grin and felt the heat in her gut spill out and race through her body like acid. She tingled from head to toe and every spot in between. And she did mean everywhere.

Holy. Shit. This man was *hot.* Seriously, insanely hot. How the hell had she not noticed *that* until right this second?

Sure, she'd thought he was attractive when she'd seen him walk into the bar. No, he wasn't the kind she typically took a second glance at. Her tastes ran more toward guys with scruffy beards and longer hair. Guys who liked to talk and did a lot of it. Mostly about themselves.

She had a reputation among her family and friends for having a radar that found the one asshole in a crowd of saints and deciding he was the one for her. Hell, even the guys she'd dated who hadn't seemed like assholes at first had turned into one faster than she could tell her sisters she'd found a decent guy. Which meant she hadn't done a lot of dating lately. Or for the past year.

Moving cross-country and starting a brand-new job a month ago hadn't helped.

She was sick of thinking maybe she'd finally found a guy who seemed decent and being disappointed once again. This guy made no attempt to hide the fact that he was only looking to get laid tonight. And that suited her just fine.

She had an itch and he looked like just the man to scratch it, even with his buttoned-up suit and his too-short brown hair and his clean shave. But his haircut showed off the rugged lines of his face and the close shave drew attention to his square jaw.

Handsome but not pretty. Masculine. Maybe a touch of caveman but not enough to make him an outright asshole. At least, not yet.

She dealt with a lot of assholes in her line of work. Most of them dressed like this guy and used their status like a weapon. Women usually dropped at their feet and they'd come to expect reverence from everyone.

This guy had taken the blonde's dismissal of him in stride. Almost as if he'd expected it. Which was ridiculous because...*damn*, he was fucking hot.

Six-foot-three, at least, a foot taller than her, with a body that made her consider climbing him like a tree. She'd wrap her arms around those broad shoulders and her legs around his waist. Then she'd press her breasts against the solid wall of his chest and—

Okay, whoa. You need to stop.

She was afraid she might drool.

She hadn't been surprised when he'd tried to pick up the blonde. She also hadn't been surprised when she'd blown him off. Such a delicate flower probably wasn't used to rough language.

She almost snorted out loud at the thought.

Her loss.

"Let's assume it was a question," she finally said. "How would you answer?"

When his grin sharpened, Tara fought the urge to grab the menu on the bar and fan herself. She wouldn't even care if anyone stared. Normally, she hated to be the center of attention. It's why she loved her job and why she was damn good at it.

Except for tonight. Tonight had been a failure. So she'd retreated to the bar for a drink before she went home. She hadn't even been thinking about meeting a guy and possibly drowning her failure in hot, sweaty, anonymous sex.

Now, it was all she could think about.

Of course, she hadn't expected to meet a guy who looked as miserable as she felt.

Usually, she would've ignored him, because any guy who hit on that blonde wasn't going to look in her direction.

And she wasn't dissing herself. Not really. She just wasn't five-eleven and built like a runway model, and she certainly didn't look like she belonged on the Norwegian ski team.

But she couldn't help laughing when he'd struck out. And when he'd turned his attention to her, she couldn't help thinking, *What the hell. Take the shot.*

And yes, she knew he wasn't looking for a date. He was looking for someone to fuck. She had no problem with that. So she'd thrown down one hell of a challenge to a man who looked like he relished them.

She met guys like him every day. Some had taken a shot at her. So far, they'd all been disappointed. For the most part, she'd gained their respect for it. It allowed her to do her job.

Of course, that meant she didn't date much because most of the guys she met were through work.

But this guy...

"How do you want me to answer?"

If he asked, she'd go home with him and spend a few hours scratching itches she hadn't known she'd had until she met him.

Sure, looks could be deceiving, but he looked like he'd be amazing in bed, even if he did seem kind of... What was the word he'd used?

Feral. From the little she knew about him, it might be the best word to describe him.

And now, he was deadly serious, those pale blue eyes of his steady on hers. Tara had a decision to make. Which wasn't really much of a decision because she'd already made up her mind.

He was going to be her consolation prize. She was giving herself permission to be bad.

She thought she saw the hint of a smile on his lips again and let herself wonder how that mouth would feel on her lips. Or on her neck. Her breasts. Her belly.

Looking closer now, she saw the faint hint of stubble on his cheeks and wondered if that would offset the softness of his lips if he worked that mouth up her legs to between them.

A shiver ran up her back as she imagined what his lips would feel like on the inside of her thighs. And higher.

And, whoa. Let's slow down just a little.

"I would want the truth."

Because she was definitely getting ahead of herself. She wasn't the kind of girl to be so damn obvious about it. At least, she never had been. Tonight, though...

She wanted what she wanted. And she wanted him.

No strings. No awkward flirting. No walk of shame. Just a night of hot, sweaty sex. Then they'd never have to see each other again. If they didn't want to.

Her sisters would roll their eyes and tell her to expect more. Her brothers would want to kill him. Her parents would never find out because they wanted to believe she was still a virgin.

"Then I guess first I'd ask if you want another drink."

She'd finished her whiskey a while ago but hadn't signaled for another because she'd been wrapped up talking to him.

Now, she nodded, not wanting to leave yet. Not when she was having more fun than she'd had in the past several months. The move back to Philadelphia had been unexpected, but when she'd been offered this job, she hadn't once considered turning it down.

It was exactly the stepping-stone she needed. But, yeah, moving here had been fraught with so many pitfalls, it wasn't funny.

She'd proven she had the ability for the position, but it was a big step, and she didn't want to fuck it up. Didn't want to give the doubters any ammunition.

And if she did mess up...

Hell, she didn't even want to think about it. She didn't want to fail and disappoint her dad.

"Sure. I'll take another."

While he signaled the bartender for another round, she considered asking his name. Then again... She wasn't sure she wanted to know.

If he was any good in bed, maybe she'd ask later. Looks could be deceiving, sure, but... This guy looked like he could provide one hell of a lot of fun for a few hours.

If she had the guts to actually follow through.

And what if he's a serial killer? Or a freak who wants to suck your toes?

Seriously, why would anyone want to suck toes? She didn't get it. But if this guy wanted to suck her toes... Hell, she might just let him.

After the bartender poured them both another drink, the guy lifted his, waiting until she'd tapped his glass to take a swallow.

"So, you want to come back to my condo?"

She managed not to choke on the alcohol as it slid down her throat, but she did cough a little as she started to laugh. She could tell from the look on his face that the words had just kind of fallen out of his mouth. Whether because he didn't know how else to say them or because he just didn't care how they sounded.

Honestly, she appreciated his candor. Much better than some slick asshole who buttered her up but didn't mean a word of it. She didn't suffer assholes well. They pissed her off.

Her sisters called her a tomboy like it was a bad thing. Her brothers accepted her as one of them, which kind of proved her sisters' point.

"For sex?"

He didn't look surprised at her blunt reply. In fact, he smiled again. He looked kind of rusty at it, like he didn't do it often.

"Yeah. If you're up for it."

Oh, she was up for it.

"And you're not a serial killer?"

His smile widened and his eyes glinted with amusement. "Nah. If I was, I wouldn't be buying you the good stuff."

Her laughter spilled out in a snort, which she quickly covered by putting her hand over her mouth. Wherever her sisters and her mom were, they were rolling their eyes and didn't know why.

"I have no idea why I'm laughing." She finally got herself under control after a few long seconds. "It wasn't that funny."

He tossed back the rest of his drink. "True. But no one usually laughs at my jokes so you get points. If I was a serial killer, I'd at least give you a head start."

"You know you're weird, right?"

Shrugging, he didn't look offended. "So people tell me. I don't typically give a shit."

"I think I like that about you."

"What? That I don't give a shit?"

She smiled. "That you're a little weird. And I don't mean weird in a bad way. People always tell me I'm weird. I just don't fit into their little boxes of personalities. Weird is the box that holds everyone who doesn't conform."

His eyes widened slightly. "That's kind of a profound thing to say at a bar at..." he checked the watch on his wrist, "close to midnight on a Monday in July."

"Is there a good time to be profound?"

"Tuesdays at noon."

He said it so matter-of-factly, she started to laugh again, inadvertently charmed.

"Then I'll be sure to keep it for then."

Not that she'd be anywhere near this man tomorrow at noon. She had a press conference to cover, one she couldn't miss, so she needed to be home by nine in the morning.

Which gave them roughly eight hours to have wild, nameless sex.

Her breath caught in her chest as she thought about all the things they could do in that amount of time.

How many times could he reasonably get it up? How many hours of sleep could she reasonably exist on? She had a feeling he'd be worth every single minute of rest she'd miss. Call it a gut feeling. And when she left his place sometime before daylight, it'd probably be with a smile.

While she thought through her answer, he watched her openly, not disguising the heat in his eyes.

Damn, he made her blush. And she wasn't even embarrassed.

She was horny. And amazingly, she'd found a guy who fit

her very narrow personality box for a sexual partner.

It was on the tip of her tongue to ask if he was ready to leave when he stood. And held his hand out to her.

Moment of truth.

Tipping her head back, she let the rest of the very good whiskey slide down her throat then set her glass on the bar next to his.

And took his hand.

He held hers while she stood but released her as soon as she was on her feet. In the few seconds they'd touched, she'd noticed his hands were rough, like he worked with them. It totally did *not* match the image of who she thought he was.

And added to his attraction.

Her lungs struggled for air as she thought about those hands against her skin. The flush on her cheeks deepened.

Grabbing her tote, she headed for the door, looking over her shoulder to make sure he was following her.

She didn't need to look far. He was by her side almost immediately, one hand low on her back. The heat of his fingers burned through her dress, just above her ass. Now standing next to him, she got a better sense of how tall he was. And how broad.

And damn, he smelled good.

She had to make a conscious effort not to trip over her own feet as they walked toward the hotel entrance. She was wearing heels and, yeah, they weren't that high, but they weren't her typical flats.

Luckily, they didn't have to walk far. Several taxis waited at the curb and he opened the door to the first one in line, let her slide in then got in after her.

And now they were closer than they'd been all night. Her heart beat practically into her throat as he leaned forward and gave the driver an address near the art museum.

It took her brain a few seconds to process that and then a few more seconds to realize his address was in an area she wouldn't be able to afford unless she won a few million in the lottery.

She bit her tongue against the urge to ask him something stupid, like what he did to be able to afford to live there.

She wanted to have sex with the guy, not marry him. Hell, she wasn't even sure she wanted to know his name.

Did he think it was weird that they hadn't exchanged names? He could've asked for hers but he hadn't. Maybe he just didn't care enough to ask. Or maybe, like her, he didn't want to burst the bubble.

As he settled into the seat next to her, their arms brushed. Such a simple act, and yet her heart started to pound like she'd run a marathon and she couldn't catch her breath. And now she became hyperaware of everything about him.

His size, the heat coming off his body...his scent. How the hell did he manage to smell so damn good? And it wasn't, like, some expensive cologne. She was pretty sure it was just soap.

Okay, you need to get a grip and not on him.

Because if she touched him now, even with the driver in the front seat with full view of them, she wasn't sure she wouldn't decide to just climb onto his lap and kiss him.

So she stared out the side window, the fingers of her right hand tapping out a nervous beat on her thigh.

At least a minute passed while she bit her tongue against the urge to say something stupid but needing to fill the silence in some way. Her brain spun in circles but couldn't come up with the right words.

Then he leaned closer, his lips only inches from her ear.

"Are you sure this is what you want?"

Oh god, *yes.*

She absolutely wanted him.

Sucking in a deep breath, she turned to face him. And found herself staring at his lips. Damn, he had a beautiful mouth.

Her breath caught in her throat and she couldn't drag her gaze away. It would only take a tiny adjustment on her part to close the distance between them and press her lips against his.

Patience. Just a little more patience.

Pulling away just enough that she could look up into his eyes, she caught him staring at her mouth before he lifted his gaze to hers.

She had to swallow before she could answer and then she could only nod because she wasn't sure she could speak coherently.

"Yes."

She thought he'd pull away, settle back into his seat, and they'd spend the rest of the drive in silence. Instead, he turned toward her more fully, one arm across the back of the seat.

"Make me believe it."

She distinctly heard the challenge in his voice and took a second to think about her answer before she let herself smile up at him.

"You have a beautiful mouth."

He hadn't been expecting that. His eyes widened and that mouth curved in a smile that made it even harder for her to breathe. Her cheeks had to be fire-engine red by now, but maybe he couldn't see that because of the darkness in the taxi.

"I want to put my mouth on your body," his voice dropped to a low rumble, "and kiss my way down to your toes."

Now her lungs froze and she wasn't sure she'd be able to draw in air.

It took her a few seconds to answer. "I have no problem letting you do that."

She was surprised her voice sounded as strong as it did, able to be heard over the sounds of the engine and the noise of the cars passing by on the street.

"What else will you let me do?"

The word "Anything" sat on the tip of her tongue but she bit it back. Didn't want him to get the wrong idea.

Although...she was in a cab on her way back to his place after meeting him in a bar and she didn't even know his name.

He probably had all sorts of very wrong but very right ideas.

Damn, girl.

Maybe she was overthinking this. She tended to do that when she was nervous.

She hadn't done this in a long time. She hadn't gone back to a guy's apartment... Hell, she hadn't had actual sex with a man in almost a year.

"Hey, you know what?" He spoke before she had a chance to say anything. "Forget I said that. I'm not really..." He sighed. "Yeah, sorry. I don't mean to be a dick."

She started to smile. "I don't think you're being a dick. I think you're kinda cute."

His mouth quirked up at one corner, which pretty much reinforced her opinion.

Then he started to laugh, low and a little growly. His laughter struck her right in her core, making her thighs clench and creating an ache low in her body that pulsed heat through her veins.

"Just kinda, huh?"

"I'm here, aren't I?"

He stopped laughing after another couple of seconds, his eyes narrowed down to slits and his mouth still holding a grin.

"Yeah. And I'm glad you are."

"Me too."

They continued to stare at each other until the taxi stopped for a red light. Then she blinked and looked out the front window.

Damn, had it gotten hotter in here? The taxi's air conditioning blew across her overheated skin but did nothing to cool her down.

She swallowed hard, her mind racing to think of something to say, anything to break the tension that had settled between them. It wasn't uncomfortable, at least not in a bad way.

But nerves had started to jangle and she had a hard time breathing. Between his nearness and the closer they got to his place, the more her lungs couldn't decide if she really needed to breathe or if she should be holding her breath. Which would lead to passing out and that would be embarrassing as hell so that probably wasn't something she should do.

Especially when she had plans to spend the next several hours having sweaty, energetic sex. She might be making a big assumption, but she was pretty damn sure this guy was going to be great in bed.

And if he wasn't? At least she could say she'd had sex with an actual guy this year.

But there was no way a guy this hot could be bad in bed. Right?

The taxi pulled up to his building and stopped. While he paid the driver, she got out and stepped onto the sidewalk. By the time she got there, he was waiting for her.

When he held out his hand, she took it and let him lead her into the building.

She was sure the lobby was beautiful. Any other time, she might've been interested in checking it out. Tonight...not so much. His hand engulfed hers in heat and scrambled her brains. She had an impression of high ceilings and glass and marble and the good life, at least a step above her own.

He steered her past security, nodding to the guard who

nodded back, and headed to the elevators that gleamed inside and out. It was a far cry from her walk-up on Bainbridge. Yeah, her place was nice and she loved the neighborhood but this... This was how the other half lived.

In the elevator, her hand still in his, she looked up at him with new eyes. Again, it was on the tip of her tongue to ask what he did for a living to be able to afford to live here. Hell, he looked like he expected her to ask.

Nope. Not gonna go there.

Instead, she turned to face him as the elevator took its own good time to reach the nineteenth floor.

"Nice place."

He nodded. "Yeah. And it's quiet."

She laughed softly. "Can't say that about my place. There's always something going on."

"You like that? Being around people?"

She had to bite back a smile. He said that like it was the worst thing in the world. Or maybe she was reading something into his words that wasn't there.

"Yeah. Sometimes. Not always." She paused, watching him watch her. "You're not a people person, are you?"

He appeared to think about that for a second, his eyes narrowing before he shrugged in a very male way. "I guess it depends on the people. My te—uh, the guys I work with, I like being around them." He shrugged. "Most of the time. Some of them piss me off a lot more than the others, but mostly they're all pretty decent. And I'm used to them."

Her reporter brain picked up on the fact that he'd hesitated over the use of one word that had sounded suspiciously like "team."

Sure, a lot of people used the word to apply to the group of people they worked with. But in her profession, a team meant something very specific.

She was beginning to believe she should know him. That she should recognize his face. That he was someone she'd seen before.

Then he leaned closer and her heart started to pound, wiping her brain clean of all thoughts other than "Is he going to kiss me? Damn, I hope he kisses me."

Her lips parted to suck in air and his gaze dropped to her lips. Seconds passed, the only sound that of the elevator gliding up to his floor. She barely noticed the chime when the elevator reached its destination, barely noticed the doors opening.

And when he didn't move right away, she parted her lips to suck in much-needed air. His gaze flashed back up to hers before he took a step back and caught the doors just before they closed again. He reached out with his free hand and waited until she took it to tug her forward, leading her out of the elevator.

No more second-guessing.

She wanted him. She was going to have him.

And she was going to have one hell of a good time doing him.

BRODY HAD the key to his apartment in his hand but he had no idea how it'd gotten there.

He couldn't remember putting his hand in his pocket to get it.

The only thing on his mind was getting this girl back to his place. His heart was racing, that's how badly he wanted her. The last time he'd been this excited about something was when the Redtails had won the Calder Cup in June.

For the past month, he'd been trying not to think about the changes happening in his world.

He'd been happy in Reading. He wasn't sure he was going to be as happy back in Philly. Had seriously considered asking his dad to let him stay. But that just wasn't going to happen. Not now, anyway.

But tonight... tonight, he was going to enjoy the hell out of this woman before everything changed.

He didn't deal well with change. Frankly it fucking sucked.

She was worth upsetting his routine. The way she stared up at him... He couldn't read her mind but he was pretty sure she was thinking the same dirty thoughts he was. And he was seriously turned on by that.

They didn't speak as they walked down the hall to his condo. The silence heightened every other sense, made him aware of how hard his heart was pounding and how tight his lungs felt in his chest.

How hard his cock was behind the zipper of his jeans.

All because of her.

He still didn't know her name and he was pretty sure he didn't want to know now. He enjoyed the anonymity. It lent an almost forbidden aspect to what was to come.

Stupid? Maybe.

Arousing? Oh hell yeah.

The light in the hall was bright enough to be annoying and he walked faster, grinning when she picked up the pace. By the time they reached his door, anticipation made his lungs struggle for air. Sucking in a breath, he fumbled the key in the lock, shoved open the door and pulled her inside.

Since he always left a light on, he had enough light to see her face. Holy shit, her expression...

Before he knew what he was doing, he reached up, framed her jaw with his hands, and held her steady.

Then he lowered his head, covered her lips with his, and kissed her like he had to or die.

As soon as their lips touched, something sparked between them. Some deep trigger that'd been waiting to be pulled. Whether it was because they were now behind closed doors and they could do what they wanted and not be constrained, he didn't know.

He only knew that the moment he put his mouth on hers, he knew neither of them would get much sleep tonight.

Their lips melded together as he tilted her head to the side. Hell, he wasn't sure who opened their mouth first. They might have done it at the same time.

She seemed just as anxious as he was to be more intimate. If he had his way, he'd strip their clothes away right now. And when there was nothing between them, he'd kiss his way down her body.

After he managed to drag himself away from her lips. Which would require a fucking huge act of will because her taste was a drug he couldn't get enough of. Sweet and hot and still tinged with the whiskey he loved.

He wanted to kiss her until he drowned himself in her.

Why her? Why now?

Why did it matter? All that mattered was keeping her right here, in front of him, where he could continue to touch her. And to make her want him as much as he wanted her.

Her lips felt like silk against his, soft and warm and pliable. And when he slid his tongue between them and into her mouth, his cock throbbed against the zipper of his pants.

Slow down, asshole. You'll scare her away.

But he didn't want to slow down. He wanted to devour her.

And she seemed more than willing to let him. Their tongues tangled, hers sliding against his and enticing him to kiss her even deeper, letting him know she was just as hot for him as he was for her.

Her hands gripped his waist, tight enough that he felt each

finger digging into his flesh just above the waistband of his pants. Ripping off his shirt so he could feel her skin on his became a burning desire that increased with every second.

Then she took a step closer, her breasts making contact with his chest, and his body reacted like a teenager locked in a clinch with his first girlfriend. Every muscle tight, every nerve ending on fire, he kissed her harder and deeper, taking everything she gave him when she opened her mouth just the slightest bit wider.

Yes. Give me everything.

That sense of challenge hit him again, the feeling that she was encouraging him, urging him to take more and wanting more for herself.

Her fingers dug more deeply into his waist and she rose onto her toes to get even closer. Sliding one hand from her jaw into her hair, he cupped the back of her head and tilted her until he had an even better angle on her mouth.

Although how the hell this kiss could get better was beyond him. He'd never had a kiss ignite like this one had.

He liked it. A lot. He liked the heat coursing through his veins and the blood throbbing in his cock. Liked the fact that he could feel the way she struggled to breathe as well. Liked that he was the one to drive her out of control.

Liked that he had to release her mouth for a second so they could both suck in air before bringing their mouths together again and going light-headed from the relief of having her mouth on his again.

He had no idea how long they stood there with their mouths crushed together. Time slipped away and had no meaning. His only immediate desire was to take as much as she'd give him.

And she gave him everything, held back nothing. He would've continued kissing her until they both collapsed against the nearest wall. And then he would've fucked her against it until they couldn't breathe.

But he didn't want to fuck her against the wall for this first time. Maybe the second or third. Maybe against the shower wall.

Maybe—

She moaned, the sound zapping through him like lightning, snapping against his control. Already at a bare minimum, the leash on his civility was about to snap.

He pulled away, forcing his eyes open, and looked down at her.

Breathing heavily, he forced himself to wait as her eyes fluttered open and she stared into his.

"Bedroom. Now."

His voice sounded rough and like a growl. Harsh and demanding. Too demanding.

Sonuvabitch. He didn't want to scare her away. He wanted her to say—

"Yes. Please."

Her voice matched his in intensity, the demand in her eyes a pull he couldn't deny.

He grinned at her use of the word "please." That one word was more of a command than anything he'd said.

"I will."

Her wide smile let him know she knew exactly what he was saying. And appreciated it.

Putting his arms around her waist, he lifted her against him. Her arms slid around his shoulders and her mouth went straight for his neck. She sucked at the tender skin right at the junction between his shoulder and neck. Heat drenched him like a downpour and his body shook like he was in the throes of a fever.

His arms tightened around her and his feet stuck to the floor as she bit her way to his ear then flicked her tongue at the lobe of his ear. How the fuck did that make him want to jump out of his skin? Electricity arced from his head throughout his entire body.

His head fell back and he panted as her lips pressed open-mouth kisses along his jaw and down to the hollow of this throat. With his eyes closed, he swore he felt everything more vividly. Felt everything more fiercely.

When she ran her tongue across his Adam's apple and to his chin, he brought his head back up, and this time he let her kiss him, let her tongue slide between his lips and tangle with his. Her hands slid from his neck, where she'd been gripping him, into his hair. Later in the season, that hair would be almost to his shoulders and she could wind her fingers around it and yank on it all she wanted.

Getting ahead of yourself, aren't you?

Probably. And he didn't fucking care.

Her kisses were all that mattered, her body a warm weight in his arms.

After a few long minutes, he broke the kiss with a groan and finally got his feet unstuck from the floor. He pointed them in the direction of the bedroom. Which was on the second floor.

He took the stairs as fast as he could, careful not to trip. But she threatened his concentration every time she flicked her tongue against his ear or her teeth along the sensitive skin just behind it.

The second time she bit his ear, he had to stop, swatting her ass barely hard enough for her to realize he'd done it.

"Do that again and we're not going to make it to the bed."

Dark eyes settled on his, a hint of a smile on her lips. "I guess as long as you're willing to be on the bottom we can do it on the stairs."

The image in his mind of her riding him right here and now made his lungs seize.

"Don't lay down a challenge you're not willing to follow through on."

Her eyebrows rose. "Who says I'm not willing to follow through? You don't know me that well."

No, he didn't. He didn't know her at all.

But he wanted her more than he'd wanted another girl. Ever.

"You're right," he answered. "But I still think we should at least attempt to make it to the bed. Not sure I want to explain why I threw out my back before—"

Shit.

He almost expected her to ask him what he'd meant to say.

When she didn't, he shook off a moment of disappointment. Which was quickly consumed by the fact that she smiled at him. An acknowledgment of his almost slip-up.

"I'm good with a bed." Then she shrugged. "Although if you don't start moving, we're never going to get there."

"Oh, we'll get there."

He'd make sure of it.

He started walking again, his only goal to get to his bedroom. But he made the mistake of glancing down at her. As their gazes connected, he knew this was more than just sex.

Worry about that tomorrow.

Right now, he wanted her naked and spread out on his bed.

Luckily, he'd remembered to put sheets on the bed when he'd gotten home yesterday.

He'd almost made it to his bedroom when her hand slid into his hair and tugged as she bit him at junction of his neck and shoulder. He'd never considered that spot an erogenous zone before this second. Now, his body reacted like she'd stuck her hand down his pants and cupped his balls.

Fire streaked through his veins before arrowing straight for his cock. Stopping in the center of the hall, only a few feet from the doorway, he sucked in a deep breath and turned his head, forcing her head up so he could capture her lips again.

The sound she made in the back of her throat was one he'd dream about for weeks. Maybe months.

Guttural and sexy as hell. She wasn't afraid to show her desire and that was such a huge fucking turn-on.

She had both hands in his hair, her nails scraping against his scalp before letting them trail down his nape and into the collar of his dress shirt. When she couldn't go any farther, she pulled back.

"Put me down."

He didn't want to put her down. He shook his head and leaned down to kiss her again.

She put one finger against his lips and lifted her eyebrows. "I promise I'll make it worth your while."

Holy fuck.

"The bed is twenty feet that way." He nodded toward the open door.

"And I promise we'll get there. Just..."

She wriggled and he set her on her feet before he lost his grip on her. He had no idea what she wanted until she pushed him back against the wall and began to unbutton his shirt.

"You have too much clothing on."

Her voice held a husky rasp that raised all the hair on his arms while his cock pressed even harder against his zipper.

"My bad. You have my permission to rip them off."

Her smile was worth every penny of what he'd have to spend to replace the suit and shirt.

"No. They're too pretty to destroy."

His lips curved in a reluctant grin. "Pretty?"

She nodded, a serious look on her face but a smile in her eye.

"Oh yes. Very pretty."

"I guess I don't care what you call them as long as you take them off."

Her gaze dropped to watch her fingers trail down the line of buttons. His gaze followed, abs clenching as she paused at the waistband of his pants. He clearly heard her indrawn breath and his own grew ragged as he waited for her to move again. Every muscle in his body tightened, anticipation and desire making his blood pump hot through his veins.

When she did, he bit back a groan of frustration when she released him and took a step back.

But before he could grab her hips and pull her back, she reached for the second button on his shirt. The first was already open. He'd undone it back at the hotel when he'd taken off his tie.

Now, she took her own damn time sliding each button through its hole with such precise movements his shirt remained closed.

When she reached the lowest button still visible above his waistband, she paused and glanced up at him.

"Don't stop now." His voice had a gruff edge to it. "You have my permission to do whatever you want."

"You sure you want to give me that much control?"

"I'll let you know when I'm going to take it back. Right now, I'm happy to let you take point."

Her lips tilted up as she tugged his shirt out of his pants. "Then I'm going to take what I want."

"Go right ahead."

Gaze narrowing, her head tilted to the side. "I have a feeling you're not usually this easy-going."

"Then you better take advantage of me while you can."

Still holding his gaze, she grabbed the sides of his shirt and spread it wide. To reveal his undershirt.

Her smiled widened. "An old-fashioned kind of guy. I like

that."

It was on the tip of his tongue to tell her he sweated too much to go without but bit it back before he embarrassed himself. Probably not something she wanted to hear.

"Just gives me another layer to remove."

As she pushed the shirt off his shoulders, he lifted his wrists for her undo the buttons there. She did and he let his shirt fall to the floor then put his hands on her waist. He wanted to start opening the line of buttons down the front of her dress but her hands were on the move again.

With her palms flat on his chest, she smoothed them up to his shoulders then back down again to his waist. Zings of sharp sensation followed her movements, making his muscles twitch in response.

His hands gripped her tighter then began to move up her sides until they were just under her breasts. But before he could start returning the favor of removing her clothes, she pulled his t-shirt out of his pants and tugged it up until he had to release her so she could take it off over his head.

She was close enough that he felt the warm exhale of her breath against his skin, making his nipples tighten in response. *Fuck.* He wanted her to put her hands on his naked chest and scrape her nails over his skin. He wanted her to mark him.

His lips parted but she beat him to the punch. She splayed her hands on his chest, her fingers brushing against his nipples before pressing both between her thumbs and forefingers. And not gently.

He sucked in a harsh breath and her eyes flew to his, widening just a little.

"Don't stop."

It sounded like the command it was. He'd legit growl if she took her hands away.

As if she'd read his mind, she curled her hands just enough

that her nails pressed against his skin as she dragged them down his chest.

Fire spread from the contact, lighting him aflame. Before she knew what was happening, he'd cupped her head in his hands and put his mouth over hers for another all-consuming kiss.

He wanted to devour her, wanted to strip her naked and feel every inch of her body pressed against his. Wanted to wrap her naked legs around his waist and sink inside her. Wanted to drown himself in her kiss and come inside her until he couldn't see straight.

Whoa. Slow down.

But she seemed to be on the same wavelength.

As her hands made their way back up his body, his went to the tie at her waist. Their tongues slid against each other in a sensuous dance while he fumbled with the buttons running the length of the dress.

Those damn little fuckers were small and his fingers were big but he finally managed to get enough of them undone so her dress hung open to just below her waist.

He subdued the urge to shout in triumph. Instead, he pulled away and let his gaze fall to her body.

"Drop the dress." Shit, that had probably sounded too much like an order. So he added, "Please."

Her smile felt like a punch to the gut. It stole his breath and made his heart try to pound out of his chest. So fucking hot.

Dropping her hands from his shoulders, she did a little twisty wiggle and that damn dress slid down her body like water and landed in a silky pile of fabric at her feet. She stood in a lace bra that left nothing to the imagination and a pair of panties that perfectly matched her skin tone.

Swallowing hard, he let himself just look at her for several long seconds.

"Beautiful."

Lifting her hands back to his body, she settled them on his waist as she leaned forward. With her lips only centimeters from his body, his lungs froze, waiting for her next move. He thought he might have to beg for her to do something, anything, when finally she settled her lips in the very center of his chest and began to explore his body with her mouth.

His cock jerked as he groaned, one hand sinking into her hair, the curls soft and tactile against his fingers. His other hand gripped her waist for several seconds before moving around to her back to bring her closer.

Their lower bodies collided, their height difference bringing his cock firmly against her stomach. His hands tightened, wanting to lift her against him so he could press his cock between her legs. He fought off the urge. He'd get to that. But first, he was going to enjoy the feel of her lips on his skin.

Kissing her way across his chest, she settled her lips around his right nipple and sucked it between her teeth. The warm, wet suction of her mouth made every nerve ending spark with desire. When her tongue flicked out to play with the hard tip, the hand in her hair clenched and tightened. He had to make a conscious effort not to pull too hard. Didn't want to hurt. More, he didn't want her to stop.

He'd never had a woman take over like she had. Most of the women he'd been with had been more than happy to let him call all the shots. He'd never realized how much he'd enjoy being on the receiving end.

Now, with her mouth exploring his chest and her hands spread across his back, he'd admit that if she shoved him against the wall and told him to stay, he'd follow her every order.

Then again, he knew his control wouldn't last forever. At some point, he was going to need to reverse their positions and cover her with his body.

As if she'd noticed his slight distraction, she bit him. Sank her teeth into his pec hard enough to sting then laved her tongue over the hurt. The combination of sensations made his stomach hollow and pushed him closer to that edge.

And then her hands went for the button on his pants.

Before he knew what he was doing, he tugged her head back and closed his mouth over hers with an almost punishing power.

He heard her suck in a surprised gasp but then she moaned low in her throat and pressed her body even closer. Rising up on her toes, she dragged her stomach up his cock until she pressed her mound against him.

That's when his control snapped.

His hands tightened on her hips and lifted her against him. She gave a little squeak as her feet left the floor but her arms wound around his shoulders and clung. Their gazes met and clung for a split second before he pressed his mouth over hers and kissed the hell out of her.

No more control. He let himself go.

Turning them, he had her back against the wall and his body plastered against hers second later.

Her arms tightened around his neck as his kiss demanded a response she seemed more than willing to give. Her hips ground against his erection, taunting him, teasing him, making him want to rip off his slacks and her panties.

But he also knew if he did that, he'd come in seconds. And that's not how he wanted her to remember him.

So he let himself kiss her for several long seconds, licking into her mouth and tangling their tongues together while his hands shifted from her waist to her ass.

She had a great ass, curvy and tight. He wanted to pet her for hours. Just thinking about it made his cock stiffen even more.

Tilting his head to get a different angle on her mouth, he held her up with one hand and let the other stroke down her thigh. She wriggled again and pressed her breasts against his chest. The slightly rough texture of her bra added an entirely new sensation that made his fingers itch to touch it.

Time to get her on the bed before he came in his pants like a teenager.

Hitching her closer, he turned and made for his bedroom. The lights of the city streamed through the window across from the bed.

Usually he closed the blackout drapes before bed but tonight, he left them open. The view looking out over Center City was spectacular but he didn't give it a glance because he only had eyes for her.

Lifting her body until she sat on the edge of the bed, she reached for him, her fingers slipping beneath his waistband and tugging him closer.

"These need to come off."

The look she gave him made him grin. It was half sweet and half sexy come-on. Combined, they made heat rush through his veins like a drug.

"Whatever you want."

Her eyebrows rose. "Are you always this compliant? No, don't answer that. Not sure I want to know. Or give you time to think about it."

"Honestly, no. Maybe you have a secret superpower you didn't know about."

Her smile spread. He fucking loved making this woman smile. It tied his stomach in knots, which normally wasn't a good thing.

Right now, though, he never wanted her to stop.

Getting ahead of yourself.

Yeah, but she had no idea what he was thinking so he could just go on thinking it.

As long as she continued to look at him that way. And continued to seduce him.

"Maybe my superpower is making your clothes disappear."

"Maybe I'm totally okay with that."

Still smiling, her fingers danced along the edge of his waistband until they reached the button. His cock was so hard, it pressed against the waistband, as if trying to get the attention of her fingers.

She very carefully worked the material so she managed to get the button through that damn hole without touching the part of him that so wanted to be touched. She took her slow, sweet time drawing down his zipper. As each tooth released, his cock pressed forward a little more and his breathing got a little rougher. And she moved just the tiniest bit closer, close enough that he felt her breath stir the trail of hair arrowing down to his cock.

Holy fuck. He wasn't sure how much more temptation he could take. Every time she breathed, his cock surged, threatening to bust through his underwear.

In the next second, he realized his hands had landed on her shoulders, his fingers digging into her warm skin before he forced himself to ease back. He didn't release her, though. He didn't want to. He wanted to pull her closer so she could put those lips on his belly, right below his navel.

But if she did, that'd be the end of him. Of course, then he could push her back on the bed and get her off with his mouth.

In fact...

She released his zipper and before she could reach into his pants to drag down his underwear, he had her flat on her back and had dropped to his knees between her thighs.

As the bed bounced beneath her, he heard her little huff of laughter and then a quick hitch of breath as he put his hands on her inner thighs.

He glanced up to make sure she was still with him. The look on her face assured him she was. Her beautiful eyes were narrowed but the slight upward tilt of her lips gave him the go-ahead.

Gliding his hands along the sleek flesh of her thighs, he soaked in the warmth of her skin for several long seconds before stopping high on her thighs. Nudging her legs a little farther apart, he brushed the tips of his fingers along the edge of her panties. Her thighs quivered but she didn't try to close her legs. Actually, she relaxed, letting her thighs drape open just a little more and allowing him even more access.

Keeping his eyes locked with hers, he slid his thumbs beneath her underwear and started to tug them down. Her breath hitched again, her thighs tensing as she lifted her butt to help him.

It took all his restraint not to rip them off but he didn't want to scare her. Still, there was such a thing as too much self-restraint. And he would never be accused of that.

He stripped her panties down her legs and dropped them. His gaze still on hers, he circled his fingers around her ankles then ran his hands from her shins to her thighs. When he finally splayed his hands on top of her thighs, he pressed them open even farther and let his gaze drop. He heard her breathe, hard and rough, but he focused his attention on her pussy. Bare and smooth, she tempted him to taste her. The hair on her mound had been trimmed short and he slid his left hand up until he could brush his thumb over it.

The sound she made in the back of her throat made him grin.

"Are you gonna do something more than touch me?"

"What? You don't like the way I'm touching you?"

"I like it. But I want more."

"More of what?"

Rising up onto her elbows, she gave him a look that perfectly expressed her thoughts. And made his grin widen even more.

"More of you making good on your promise."

"Which promise was that?"

"The one where you make me come multiple times before you get off."

He loved the sound of that. "I don't remember making that exact promise." He brushed his thumb over her mound again, this time letting it dip closer to her clit.

Her smile disappeared as she bit into her bottom lip. She had the most amazing mouth, full and quick to smile. So fucking soft.

"But it sounds like fun."

Turning his head, he pressed his lips against her right thigh, felt her entire body tremble. Her reaction made him bound and determined to deliver on that promise she said he'd made.

But first...

Dragging his lips up her thigh, he slid his hands from her thighs to just under her breasts. The bra needed to come off. Luckily for him, it hooked in the front. Working the clasp open, he pushed the two sides of the bra apart, releasing her breasts. Covering them with his hands, he squeezed the firm mounds, lifting his lips from her body so he could look into her eyes.

Her chest rose and fell in a rush, her breasts warm against his skin, firing his lust and making his heart pound. Rising up onto his haunches, he brushed his lips against the softest skin at the junction of her leg and hip and felt her body shake. Her restraint showed in the taut muscles of her stomach and the way her fingers clutched at the quilt on his bed.

He wanted to break that restraint and make her writhe.

Continuing his way up her body, he stopped to press kisses

at her belly button then made his way up the center of her body until his lips rested directly between her breasts.

Looking up at her, he grinned at the hazy look in her eyes. Good. He wanted her under his control.

"Are you ready to come? It's not going to take much this first time."

"You're pretty sure of yourself, aren't you?'

"I feel you shaking. The heat coming off your body." He deliberately glanced down. "I can sme—"

"Shut up and just do it." Her voice held a definite growl. "Or I'll think you're all talk and no action."

"Oh, honey, you have no idea."

TARA SUCKED IN AIR, fairly certain she'd almost come just from the way he called her honey.

And the smile on his face.

It shouldn't be possible. She'd never orgasmed simply from the sound of a man's voice.

Still, here she was, panting on his bed, her core clenching and hypersensitive. If he touched her clit right now, she would come. But he didn't seem to be in any hurry now to push her over the edge.

Instead, he grinned down at her, his hands still molding her breasts. She wanted him to pinch her nipples, to suck them into his mouth and make her crazy. Hell, she was already halfway there now.

"Then why don't you tell me what you're planning. Or do you need some help with that?"

She couldn't help needling him. Wanted to rock his world just as much as he was rocking hers. But he seemed to be holding all the power right now.

"Now, where's the fun in that?"

His voice made her shiver, damn him. His hands slid from her breasts to press into the bed at her sides, letting his head hang a little closer to hers. Their lips were a breath apart, his eyes boring into hers, intensely dark and focused.

She wanted him to kiss her. *Needed* him to kiss her. But he was making her wait for it. Her chest got tight and her thighs clenched. And her core ached.

"I think we'd be having a lot more fun if you were completely naked."

Reaching for his pants, she shoved them down and over his hips. She knew she wouldn't be able to get them down over his thighs without help but she didn't need them to be completely gone. She just needed a little more room to work...

Breaking his gaze, she looked down, the light from the city filtering through the window more than enough to see he wore tight, dark boxer briefs. And they showed off a very impressive bulge.

Reaching for him, she put her palm flat against that hard ridge. The heat of his body seared her skin and the sound he made low in his throat made her nipples tighten. His gaze slid to her breasts, and as she watched, he lowered his head to take one tight, sensitive nipple into his mouth.

She bit back a cry as he sucked on her, his teeth nibbling at the tip just to the point of pain. Sharp, hot lust flooded her veins and she squeezed his cock in a tight grip. Thrusting into her hand, he brought one hand up to play with her unattended breast and proceeded to drive her crazy.

Playing with her breasts with his teeth and his hands, he took her amazingly close to the edge but always drew back before he pushed her over it. Her hips lifted to rub her mound against his cock, which she continued to stroke through his underwear.

"You really need to be naked."

Her voice sounded harsh in the darkened room, almost unrecognizable to her. It would've been embarrassing how hot she was for him if he wasn't right there with her. But he was. She felt the leashed tension in his body, the way his hand tightened around her breast and the lash of his tongue against her nipple.

When he finally drew back to look into her eyes again, she could barely focus on his face.

"Hold that thought."

Before she could figure out what he was doing, he pulled away to stand. She totally embarrassed herself when she made a sound that was so close to being a whimper, she wanted to groan.

He must have heard her because his lips curved into a grin, but she forgot it in the next second when he shoved his pants and underwear to the ground in a quick motion that made her gasp for no reason other than excitement.

Then she got her first look at the completely naked man standing between her legs at the side of the bed and now she couldn't catch her breath. It seemed stuck somewhere between her lips and her chest and she sucked in another to be sure she didn't pass out. Which was a very real possibility.

Ridiculous, yeah, but she was so freaking turned on right now, she wouldn't be surprised. She'd be embarrassed as all hell but... Damn, the man was insanely good-looking and his body...

She'd never seen a body like this on anyone but an athlete.

She could practically hear her brain trying to make connections, but her synapses were fried. They must have gone up in flames the second his pants hit the ground.

In the two seconds it took this entire conversation to run through her mind, he kicked off his shoes and his pants, gripped her under arms to move her more into the center of the bed, then got onto the bed with his knees between her thighs.

Stretching her legs wide, he came down to rest his hands on the bed just above her shoulders, their eyes level.

In the next second, he closed the few inches between their lips and kissed her again. This time, there was a promise in his kiss, one she definitely wanted him to fulfill.

Her hands reached for his shoulders as he broke away from her mouth to kiss his way back down her body. He seemed to enjoy every inch of her, his lips hot and mobile on her skin.

This time, he didn't stop at her breasts but continued straight to her mound. He didn't even pretend to ask permission now.

With one hand on her mound, he deliberately spread her open with his fingers until he'd exposed her clit. His warm breath stirred the trimmed hair on her mound and made her ache with anticipation.

She almost expected him to make her wait, to torment her even more. So when he leaned forward and put his mouth over her clit and flicked at it with his tongue, she nearly screamed. Instead, she turned her head to the side and stifled it with one arm while she sank her other hand into his short hair.

His fingers felt like a red-hot brand against the inside of her thighs, his lips and tongue teasing her clit until she thought she wouldn't be able to take any more. And still, she wanted more. She felt empty and achy and so fucking horny it wasn't funny.

Wriggling closer, she needed more. More pressure, more pleasure, more pain. Every few seconds, he'd scrape his teeth across that little bundle of nerves, just enough to make her want more. Almost immediately, he'd pull back and use his tongue to soothe her. Which did nothing more than stoke the ache deep inside.

She thought she might actually start screaming if he didn't

give her what she wanted.

And then, as if he'd flipped a switch, he narrowed his focus, gave her clit one last swipe with the flat of his tongue, and slid a finger inside her slick channel to tease her.

Her sex clamped around his finger as she came, her muscles tightening in a response unlike any she'd ever had to a man before.

Starbursts flashed behind her eyelids as she gasped, her body overtaken by the intensity of her orgasm.

Seconds later, when she could breathe again, she opened her eyes and glanced down, releasing her fingers from his hair. She must've hurt his scalp, she'd been pulling so hard. But the look on his face held no pain, only the promise of more pleasure.

She still couldn't breathe right but she wanted more. Now. Wanted him to fill the empty space inside her.

Rising up onto her elbows again, she lifted a hand and crooked her index finger at him.

He rose onto his knees above her, his cock standing away from his body, hard and ready. Perfectly proportioned for his body. Long, sturdy, and making her mouth water.

She sat all the way up and reached for him, wrapping her hands around the shaft, feeling the heat and the rigid flesh. Wanting to taste him. One hand cupped his balls while the other stroked from the root to the tip.

He had turned toward the bedside table but he paused, just breathing and watching her play with him. Every upward stroke was almost punishingly tight while the downward stroke was much more a caress designed to prime him to blow.

As she watched, the head of his cock darkened to maroon and a tiny drop of precum escaped on her next upward sweep. Rubbing her thumb over the tip, she spread the silky fluid over his hot flesh. Just the simple act made her heart pound double time.

"I'm clean."

Amazingly, she trusted him.

"You're still going to need that condom. In a minute."

She caught a brief glimpse of his grin before she leaned forward and took him in her mouth. As her lips slipped over his head, she sucked him in, the salty heat of his skin enticing her to take him deeper. With one hand, she played with his balls. With the other, she held him steady.

Not that he seemed to be going anywhere. One hand wove through her curls, not directing her or forcing her. Just holding her.

The other landed on her shoulder, where he let his fingers play over her skin before sliding down to her breasts and pinching the nipple of one between his fingers.

The stimulation on her already overly sensitive nipples was enough to make her moan around his cock. Which he seemed to like, if his answering groan was any indication. And the slight thrust of his hips.

He caught himself before he forced his cock farther into her throat. Pulling back to the tip, she looked up at him and released him, kissing the tip before blowing a cool stream of air against his overheated flesh.

His beautiful body tightened, his jaw clenching and those beautiful eyes narrowing down to glittering slits of gray.

"Suck me. Please."

She had a feeling this man didn't use that word a lot. Her stomach fluttered in response, gooseflesh covering her skin.

Then she closed her eyes and gave herself over to the pleasure of pleasing him.

The sounds he made let her know exactly what he liked and what he didn't. Not that he didn't like much. He didn't like when she pulled away, but she figured turnabout was fair play.

He loved when she took him in almost to the root then

sucked, hard. He loved when she swirled her tongue around the tip then flattened it and slid it along the shaft.

His labored breathing filled the room as she pushed him closer and closer to the edge. She wondered if he'd let her finish him like this, with her mouth, but as soon as she had the thought, he pulled away.

When she made a little sound of disappointment, he made a noise deep in his chest and pushed her onto her back on the mattress.

Again, he loomed over her but now he had a condom in his hand and just the thought that he was about to fuck her made her swallow. Hard.

Her legs spread open a little more, one hand splayed over her stomach, the other open and spread out on the bed next to her head.

With his eyes on hers, he tore open the condom but as soon as he started to roll it onto his cock, she let her gaze fall down his body. His big hands took care of job quickly but it made her mouth water to see him handle himself. She had the brief thought that she wanted to watch him jerk himself off. But not now. Definitely not now.

She ached and her hand drifted lower, catching his attention. Her clit needed to be stroked but she wanted him inside her while she did.

"Now."

She could barely hear her own voice but he obviously heard her just fine.

"Hold yourself open. I want to see you touch yourself."

Sliding both hands to her hips, she opened her pussy to him, lifting her hips to entice him closer. It worked. He moved forward, settling onto his hands and knees above her, before lowering his hips until his cock brushed against her lower lips. Pulling her hand away, she grabbed his hips and tried to make him move. It was like trying to move a mountain. She couldn't do it.

Instead, he leaned down and settled his mouth over hers, kissing her with an intensity that stole her breath. When she moaned and thrust her mound against him, he put a little more of his weight on her, effectively holding her still.

She wanted to complain but she didn't want to stop kissing him. Wanted to tell him to stop messing with her but wanted him to continue all night.

Then he moved his hips and began to sink into her.

She swore her heart stopped as his cock pushed inside, spreading her wide, making her tighten around him as he sank deeper with every breath. She tried to lift her hips to get him to give her more, but he was too heavy. His hips pinned hers against the bed, frustrating her with the inability to move.

With his mouth over hers, she couldn't tell him to move, to hurry, to fuck her harder. Instead, her increasing frustration simply fueled her desire. Heat raced through her veins, pooled in her gut and between her legs.

Now with both hands on his hips, she let her nails sink deep into his flesh, pulling him closer. At least, she tried to pull him closer.

Damn him, it wasn't working. His cock had barely breached her and now he released her mouth so he could pull back and look down at her.

"Move, damn you."

His lips curved in a wickedly sexy grin at her growly demand. But she saw sweat beading at the temples and felt the tension in his body. The man wasn't as in control as he liked to front.

"I am moving."

"Not fast enough."

He shook his head, as if he was trying to clear his thoughts.

"I like hearing you beg."

"I'm not begging." She refused to. Besides, this was the most fun she'd had in bed…ever. "I'm demanding."

"I don't think you're in any position to demand anything."

As part of the very sexy game they were playing, he couldn't have said anything guaranteed to make her want him more. Her body went liquid beneath his, her breath rushing from her lungs past her lips. As if that were the sign he'd been waiting for, his hips snapped against hers, lodging him deep inside her.

Her eyes closing, she moaned as he ground against her, doing some slow circle with his hips that managed to massage her clit and push her closer to another orgasm. Just when she thought he might actually tip her over, he pulled out.

His neighbors could probably hear her frustrated groan. At least she made him respond with a sharp, indrawn breath when she dug her nails into his flanks again and lifted her mouth to his chest and bit him on his left pec.

His hips flexed as he thrust deep, and then he couldn't seem to stop. Her head hit the mattress, quickly followed by his as he covered her mouth and kissed her hard and deep.

Her legs wrapped around his waist and her hands moved up his back to his shoulders. Then she held on for the ride.

BRODY LOST IT. He fucking lost his mind when she bit him and he wasn't sure he totally regained it as he let his body take over.

He fucked her, hard and fast, and he wasn't sure he would've heard a bomb blast outside the door. Every molecule of his body was focused on her.

Her taste flooded his mouth as his tongue danced around hers, sucking the sweetness out of her. Every inch of skin where they touched felt like it was on fire. They were both sweaty and their flesh clung.

And her pussy tightened around him until he thought he wouldn't be able to pull out. He didn't want to pull out. Not ever. He wanted to fuck this girl until neither of them could move or see straight.

Her every move made his cock harder. Every sound made it harder for him to breathe. He wasn't sure his heart had ever pounded harder at practice.

He couldn't get enough of her. Each passing second brought a new and amazing sensation.

Slow down.

Fuck no. He couldn't stop. He wanted to push her over the edge again. Needed to make her come again.

On his next inward thrust, he paused again for a few seconds, grinding against her clit, making her moan into his mouth.

He wanted to beat his chest in victory at the way she clung to him, her legs tightening around his waist as she spread her hands across his back then raked her nails down the entire length of his spine.

The sting of her nails combined with the silky heat of her arms and legs made his cock twitch and his balls draw up tight.

Tearing his mouth away from hers, he pressed his lips against her temple as she gasped in air.

"Don't stop. Don't stop."

He had no intention of stopping, but the sound of her voice acted like a cattle prod to his desire.

He withdrew again then fucked her hard and fast, nailing her into the bed. Until finally, she turned her head and bit his neck and he released into her with a groan that practically shook the walls.

THREE

"Whoa. Tara. You look like you had a good night. Wanna share with the class?"

"Nope. I'm late."

Tara knew she could barely be understood as she mumbled around the half of a bagel clenched in her teeth. She also knew Ethan Reidenour understood her anyway.

"I overslept and I can't be late to the damn presser."

Ethan's raised eyebrows made it clear he wasn't backing down. He didn't care that she needed to get over to the arena for the press conference. "Uh-huh. You're not getting off the hook that easily, you know that, right?"

Tara gave Ethan the finger as she dumped her bag on her desk, trying really hard not to spill her industrial-size coffee while she did. She totally needed that coffee to function this morning. Without it, she'd be a zombie. A happy, sated zombie who was sore between her legs. But who wouldn't be good for much more than staring blindly into space while she thought about how she'd gotten to be so tired and why exactly she was sore in all the right places.

And that couldn't happen. Not today. She needed to be

functional.

Ethan sat forward, crossing his arms on his desk, gaze narrowed on her. "Okay, now I know something's up. Come on, you've got a few minutes before you need to leave. Tell me. Did you actually get laid last night? You're smiling like you got laid last night."

She slid Ethan a sidelong glance before dropping into her chair at her desk across from his. She had just enough time to finish her coffee and bagel, make sure her phone was fully charged so she could record interviews if she needed to, and that she had a couple reporters' notepads and a few of her favorite pens and mechanical pencils in her bag.

"No comment." Another bite of bagel. "There may be a formal statement later."

Ethan's low laugh had the power to make straight women and gay men sigh with desire. For some reason, she was immune. Except to Ethan's powers of persuasion.

"Now, you know I'm not going to have the patience to wait until later. Hell, it doesn't matter. I know you did." Leaning back with a grin, he rapped his knuckles against the desktop. "Good for you, babe. You needed to get that frustration out of your system."

She considered sticking her tongue out at him then thought better of it. But he wasn't wrong. Ethan was pretty much never wrong.

"I can neither confirm nor deny." She looked at him over the top of the low wall that separated their desks. "But I will say I didn't get much sleep last night."

Tara heard the distinct sound of plastic wheels on laminate flooring and looked up to see Lindsay Plekanik rolling across the aisle to lean against Ethan's desk.

"So you did get laid last night." Lindsay held out her fist to bump knuckles with Ethan then with Tara. "Good on you, dude. Someday maybe I'll actually enjoy sex again." She sighed, sounding only slightly dramatic. "Not that I don't love my husband, but when you have kids, they become instant birth control."

With a sigh, Tara leaned back in her chair and glared at her friends. Okay, she tried to glare, but last night's sex had made her stupid, apparently. All she wanted to do was brag about how many times she'd orgasmed and how good it had been.

Ethan leaned back in his chair, devastating grin on full display. The man looked like a fashion model, had the wardrobe to match, and hid a huge heart under those fancy clothes. If it wasn't so adorable, she would totally rag him on it constantly. But unlike her, he was totally serious about finding the love of his life. Tara wasn't sure she believed in that particular fairy tale.

What she did believe in was finding joy where you could get it. And last night, she'd found it in bed with a man whose name she didn't know.

Lindsay would totally understand.

Even though the other woman was ten years older and happily married with two kids, Lindsay had a sailor's vocabulary and ink in her veins. When the police chief saw her coming on rounds, he'd been known to hide. Seriously. He'd barricade himself in his office and tell his secretary not to disturb him under penalty of termination. Cops scattered when Lindsay had a lead on a story because they knew she wouldn't stop until she found out what she needed to know.

She was a one-woman bulldozer who looked a little like Reese Witherspoon and had the accent to match. And she instilled fear in men who routinely faced death every day.

Shaking her head, Tara looked around the newsroom, thankfully mostly deserted on this side. There were a few copy editors and editors on the opposite side of the floor, hunched over their keyboards, staring at their screens, showing no interest in what was going on over here.

Good.

Leaning forward on her desk, she released her grin.

"Oh my god, you guys. It was so good."

Ethan snorted, crossed his arms over his chest and waited for more. Lindsay maneuvered her chair over to Tara's side of the cubicle for better cross-examination position.

"Are we talking multiple-orgasm good or just, 'It's been so long, I finally had sex' good?"

Tara leaned closer and made an insanely ridiculous noise somewhere between a squeal and sigh. "I'm talking multiples, and let me just say the guy knows how to use his mouth."

Ethan rolled his eyes and shook his head, but Tara saw his amusement on his perfect face.

Lindsay wasn't as controlled.

"Holy shit. A goddamn unicorn. I hope to hell you tied him to your bed so he can't get away. Damn, girl, when do you see him again?"

Tara's nose wrinkled and Ethan leaned closer, his eyes narrowing as he picked up on what she wasn't saying. "What's that face for?"

Tara considered shoving the bagel in her mouth again but she knew he'd just wait her out.

"I never got his name."

Ethan's mouth dropped open but no sound came out. And the look on his face would be priceless if it wasn't for the fact that Lindsey practically screeched "What?" loud enough for people on the other side of the city to hear her.

Okay, of course it wasn't that bad, but damn, it was close.

Looking over her shoulder at the editing center, where a few people had turned to find out what was going on, she turned back to Lindsay and Ethan with a scowl.

"Jeez, Lins, I don't want the entire newsroom to know my business. I've got enough people looking over my shoulder already."

Lindsay looked suitably cowed for all of two seconds. Then her mouth opened for more interrogation but Ethan beat her to the punch.

"Does he know who you are?"

She shook her head. "It was perfect. Honest to God. He didn't turn out to be a serial killer or a pervert and he didn't hurt me and, oh my god, it was freaking amazing. Like something out of a book, you know? I mean, we talked for about an hour at the bar before we went back to his place. I swear I thought I was gonna melt in the car on the way."

"Wait? So you know where he lives?" Lindsay got a huge grin on her face. "Then we can look—"

"No." Tara shook her head. "No way. That would totally be an invasion of privacy."

"Babe, I think your privacy was pretty well invaded last night."

If she'd had something other than her bagel in her hand, Tara would've thrown it at Ethan, but she couldn't help laughing at his droll delivery. Ethan did dry, biting wit better than anyone she knew.

"You know what I mean." She added an eyeroll for effect. "If he'd wanted me to know his name, he would've told me. And if I'd wanted him to know mine, I would've told him."

"Who the hell do you think you are?" Lindsay shook her head. "Fucking Cinderella? Did you lose your glass slipper *and* your marbles last night? How are you going to find him again?"

It was on the tip of her tongue to say she didn't want to see him again, but that would probably be a lie. Because, holy hell, last night had been...awesome.

Then she shook her head because she knew, *she knew*, that

if she saw him again and the next time didn't live up to last night, it'd be ruined for her.

And if it got better?

She sighed. No, life just didn't work like that. At least not for her.

"No, I get it." Ethan spoke up before she had a chance. "It was a fantasy. What if he doesn't live up to it in the light of day?"

Now she did take another bite of her bagel as she touched the tip of her nose and nodded at Ethan.

Lindsay sat back in her chair with a huff. "All right, I guess I get your point. But isn't there a little part of you that wants to see him again?"

Shrugging, she continued to chew her bagel so she wouldn't have to answer right away. But finally, she couldn't stop herself.

"I think...maybe, yeah. And then I remind myself that he'd probably turn out to be just like all the rest of the men I've ever dated. Dicks."

Lindsay snorted while Ethan nodded in agreement.

"Sometimes," Lindsay sighed, "I think I got the last decent man around."

"Lins, if I had the chance, I'd steal Mark away from you without a care for you or your adorably heathen children." Ethan turned back to Tara with a grin. "But yeah, for some reason, you seem more susceptible to douchebags. Which I know is why you haven't dated since you moved here. I mean, I get it, but maybe you should've at least gotten this one's name. Hopefully there were no hidden cameras and you don't end up on Pornhub."

Tara had a momentary freak-out then shook her head.

"No. Nuh-uh. Won't happen. He just didn't give off that vibe, you know? He seemed like a an honest-to-god decent person."

"One you're never gonna see again," Lindsay added.

Since the thought was starting to bring down her high, Tara waved a hand in front of her, as if that could just erase everything her so-called friends had said in the past few minutes.

If she were less mature, she'd stick her fingers in her ears and sing, "Lalalala" until she had to leave for the presser.

Which, she checked the time on her watch, was in a couple of minutes.

"All right, you two. Now that you've managed to make me regret telling you what happened, I need to leave."

"You want to get dinner tonight?" Ethan asked while she swallowed the rest of her bagel and washed it all down with coffee. "I certainly don't have anything to do and Aunt Rose has been a little more...difficult lately."

Ethan lived in half a duplex in Fishtown and his elderly aunt lived in the other. The building had been owned by his parents before they'd moved to Florida and left it to Ethan, with the stipulation that his father's sister remain until she died or Ethan had her committed, which he'd come close to doing more than once.

"Sure. We'll talk when I get back."

If his aunt was giving him trouble, Ethan probably needed to talk and wouldn't want to do it here. There were still a few people in the newsroom who gave him grief because he was gay but they were passive-aggressive and he didn't let it bother him. Mostly. On a really bad day, his aunt could be amazingly homophobic. On her good days, she loved him like a son. Yes, Alzheimer's sucked.

"Oh, to be young and have disposable income and no ties." Lindsay sighed dramatically as she rolled herself back to her side of the aisle.

"Yeah, yeah. Just remember you did it to yourself, Lins." Tara got up to get another notebook before she had to leave.

"You could say the same thing about yourself, Tare."

Five minutes later, in a taxi on her way to the Broad Street Arena for the Colonials press conference, Tara thought about Lindsay's parting shot.

She'd made a conscious decision not to find out the guy's name. There'd been plenty of times she could've just come right out and asked. And yet she hadn't.

Because it totally would've ruined the fantasy.

But now...

Would it have killed you to find out before you snuck out the door this morning?

And did she really want to see him again?

If someone had asked her that question last night, she would've said no. And it might have been true.

This morning... This morning she'd wimped out. There'd been a moment—

Okay, at least be honest with yourself.

There'd been several times she'd wanted to ask and couldn't bring herself to do it. And if she hadn't snuck out the damn door when he was in the shower, maybe she'd know it know.

What were the odds of running into the guy again?

Better if she started to hang out at Haven, the hotel from last night. It definitely wasn't one of her usual haunts, but she was sure Ethan would be up for a visit every now and then.

The friends she'd made in her building would think she was crazy. Most of them never went as far north as Rittenhouse Square. Why would they when South Philly had more than enough places to keep them occupied? And if they got bored, they'd head out to Fishtown or Manayunk. They didn't play in Rittenhouse Square.

She was pretty sure her mystery man from last night was pretty damn comfortable in those circles.

With a heavy sigh, she forced herself not to think about him anymore and turned her attention instead to the press conference.

This was what she should be focusing on. Her job. She'd only been with the *Record* for a few weeks, hired for a general sports assignment beat. But the Phillies beat reporter had made it clear he was retiring at the end of the year and there'd be a spot open to cover baseball. Two reporters covered the major league team. She wanted to be one of them when the spot became available.

The sports editor had told her when he'd hired her that she was going to be covering baseball and basketball, but since the Colonials regular reporter, Sean Simmons, was on medical leave for a torn rotator cuff, she had to cover Duncan Mitchell's first press conference as the new Colonials general manager.

Last week, she'd lost a game of rock-paper-scissors to Charlie Hawkins and Will Russo, the other general assignment sports reporters, over who had to cover the press conference today. Last night had been a futile attempt on her part to get a jump on the story. She'd heard about the private party and had gone to the hotel on the off chance she might get to talk to Mitchell. That hadn't happened but she'd ended up with one hell of a consolation prize.

Today, though, she had to be on her game.

She was a damn good writer. She wouldn't have gotten this job if she wasn't. But the fact that her dad had been one of the best sportswriters this paper and this city had ever seen meant she had to work twice as hard to prove she was half as good.

Her dad now made a killing writing sports biographies and she'd been hired, not to take his place, because honestly, she didn't have the skill her dad had honed after more than thirty years on the job, but because she was good at what she did.

After three years on the west coast covering major league and college baseball for a couple of mid-size papers and slowly making a name for herself, she'd finally gotten the opportunity to return home and work for the paper she'd grown up idolizing.

Maybe I was wrong not to get his name.

The more she thought about it, the more she thought, yeah, she'd been ridiculously wrong. And not just wrong but stupid.

She couldn't stop thinking about him. Every now and then, her brain would flash a picture of him naked, staring at her with those dark eyes as he rode her to another orgasm.

Or she'd get a flash of his smile. He hadn't smiled a lot, but when he did, she felt like she'd won the freaking lottery.

She had a feeling they were a lot more alike than she'd realized last night.

With a huff, she chewed herself out for not getting his name until the taxi stopped in front of the arena on Broad Street.

"Who goes to bed with a guy and doesn't get his name?"

She muttered that under her breath so no one would hear her, although there weren't many people in the area. She'd arrived a good fifteen minutes earlier than she needed to, just so she wouldn't be late. You could never tell with Philly traffic. Better early than never.

She'd introduce herself to whatever Colonials organization members happened to be around before the press conference. Not that she expected to see much of them. Her focus on baseball and basketball meant she wouldn't cover much, if any, hockey.

But you couldn't go to Boston College and not graduate with an appreciation for the sport. She'd covered more than a few games for the school newspaper during her four years there.

Walking through a side entrance, she checked in with security then headed for the nearest bathroom to make sure she didn't look like she felt. The temperature outside hovered just above ninety and the humidity had to be close to a hundred percent. Her hair probably looked like she'd stuck her hand in an electrical socket.

Looking in the mirror, she sighed and wrinkled her nose at her reflection. Not too frizzy, just a lot more curl than normal. She wished she could be one of those girls who embraced the wave. She would it if weren't so psycho most days.

Satisfied that the little bit of mascara she'd applied this morning hadn't run like rats from a sinking ship and that she hadn't chewed off her tinted lip balm, she sighed at the dark circles under her eyes. Couldn't do anything about those. Besides, she grinned at her reflection, she'd had a hell of a lot of fun getting those dark circles.

Too bad you don't know his name.

Sticking her tongue out at her reflection, she headed back out and made her way to the media room. Turned out she wasn't the only reporter who'd arrived early.

She nodded to the guy who'd grabbed a seat in the second row, probably only a couple years older than her, who looked up for a second to acknowledge her presence before putting his head down over his phone again.

Another guy was from one of the TV network affiliates. She recognized his face. He did a double take before grinning at her. She'd been warned about him by every female sports reporter in Philly. He'd been compared unfavorably to a dog and a snake by every single one of them.

She nodded at him before turning away and scoping out the rest of the room.

Out of the corner of her eye, she saw someone approaching.

"Ms. Downey? Hi, I'm Gabrielle Mitchell, director of media relations for the Colonials. I wanted to introduce myself and say welcome to Philadelphia. It's nice to meet you."

Tara stood to greet the woman and immediately wished she'd worn heels. At five-three, she was at a serious height disadvantage with this completely-put-together woman with her white blouse, black slacks, and perfectly straight, perfectly highlighted golden-brown hair.

If Tara ever fell for a woman, she was pretty sure this one would be high on the list.

"Thank you." She took Gabrielle's outstretched hand, hoping like hell that hers wasn't sweaty. Ugh, she was a mess today. "Please, call me Tara. I'm excited to be here."

The woman's smile seemed genuine enough. Still, Tara knew how fast that smile could turn cold or distant when she needed to ask tough questions.

"I have to say it'll be nice to have a female in the media pool occasionally." Gabrielle had leaned in a little and her grin seemed even more open now. "It's been a boys club for so long, sometimes I think I get testosterone poisoning. So please, let me know if you need anything at all."

Then she handed over the large envelope she'd been holding. "Your credentials. And my business card with my cell number. Don't hesitate to call with any questions."

"I won't. Thanks."

Tara expected the other woman to move on then, but Gabrielle leaned even closer. Not enough to make Tara feel threatened or encroached upon, just curious.

"I know this is probably totally inappropriate but I'm gonna say it anyway."

Now Tara's eyes widened and she hoped she didn't look as wary as she felt. Usually when people prefaced something like this with those words, it wasn't anything good.

"I only got to speak with your dad a couple of times when I first took over this position before he retired. But I just wanted to say, he was an amazing guy. His writing is top-notch and he was always a professional. I had a totally professional crush on your dad." Gabrielle shook her head, her cheeks actually burning a little. "And that's probably *way* more than you ever wanted to know."

Tara chuckled, relieved. "Honestly, you're not the first person to say that to me, although usually it's a guy. So trust me, you're not the first or the worst."

Gabrielle let her head fall back as she laughed, and for a split second, Tara thought the other woman looked familiar. She had no idea who Gabrielle reminded her of but she wrote it off as just one of those things. Everyone had a doppelganger, right?

When Gabrielle finished laughing, she held out her hand again and shook Tara's. "Thank you. And I'm sorry if that was TMI, but even though your dad didn't cover hockey often, he was well liked around here. Just wanted you to know. I'm sure we'll talk again soon. Nice to meet you, Tara. And seriously, if you need anything, please ask. The boys club is still tight in professional sports. Don't let them intimidate you."

Gabrielle turned and walked toward the door near the small stage set up for the speakers.

Tara was still smiling when someone tapped her on the shoulder from behind.

Looking over her shoulder, she nodded to Liam, the *Record* photographer who was covering the event. The guy was only a year younger than her but looked like he was twelve. He probably got laid more than anyone in the newsroom, which was kind of weird but whatever.

He'd asked her out two days after she'd started and she'd been on the verge of asking him for his ID when Lindsay had stepped in and saved her from embarrassing herself.

She'd still had to say no because she just couldn't date a guy who looked like he hadn't graduated from high school.

"Met the Ice Princess, I see. She's tough. Word of advice? Don't get on her bad side. She'll freeze you out."

Tara tossed Liam a knowing look over her shoulder. "Get turned down, huh?"

To his credit, Liam grinned and shrugged. "Doesn't mean I'm not right. Cross her at your peril."

Tara didn't answer because another reporter passed in front of her to sit in the second row, followed by another photographer. Seconds later, more than half of the chairs in the room were filled.

She took a few seconds to get the recorder app open on her phone and just as she got it started, the door to the rear of the stage opened and people started to file out.

First out were the assistant coaches, Domenic Mann and Gary Ellis, then head coach Angstadt and two of the team's owners. Taking out the press materials Gabrielle had given her to see if it included their names, she didn't see the faces of the next two men who sat at the table.

Her gaze flicked to the door to see Gabrielle close it behind her.

Then she looked up at the table.

And felt all the blood rush to her head.

Someone had started to talk but she couldn't understand a word they were saying.

All she could hear was the rush of blood in her ears and the voice of doom in her head.

Because the man sitting next to the Colonials' new general manager, who was the reason she was here today, was the man she'd had amazing sex with last night.

A man whose name, according to the placard in front of him, was Brody Mitchell.

Colonials defenseman and son of the new general manager.

Oh fuck.

FOUR

The look on the woman's face as she stared at Brody said it all. She was just as surprised to see him as he was to see her.

The wide dark eyes and parted lips. The furious blush on her cheeks.

Yep. She was shocked as shit.

No one would ever accuse him of being a master at reading people, mainly because he usually didn't give a shit what other people were thinking unless they were his coach, his dad, or his mom. Sometimes his sister and brother.

But he knew that shock wasn't fake. So last night hadn't been planned.

But... Holy *shit*. She was a *reporter*? A goddamn reporter who covered his fucking *team*?

No. No way. It couldn't be. He'd never seen her before.

What the fu—

Beneath the table, Gabby kicked his left shin with the pointy toe of her shoe.

It was enough to get him to stop staring at his mystery woman for long enough to glance at his sister, who pointedly looked down at the table in front of him.

What the hell—

A piece of paper lay on the table with words written on it.

He shook his head to get his brain to settle back into its normal spot, while his heart continued to pound like he'd just been laid out by Francois Villenueve, one of the league's hardest hitters.

Blinking, he forced himself to read it. His sister had written five words.

DUDE SNAP OUT OF IT

Shit.

Flashing another glance at his sister, he gave a barely noticeable nod, then forced himself to pay attention to the press conference. You know, the one where they were introducing his father as the new general manager of the team he played for.

Fuck.

He hoped like hell no one else had noticed his momentary lapse of sanity. He didn't want to call attention to himself. At least, he didn't want to call any more attention to himself. The press was going to do it for him.

But now all he could think about was her.

Who the hell was she?

While he tried to get his heart to beat in a normal rhythm and get a handle on whatever the hell Coach Angstadt was saying, he deliberately didn't let himself look in her direction.

Whoever she was.

He needed to find out her name. And he knew exactly who to ask.

"Thank you all for coming," his dad said. "It's great to be back here where it all started for me."

Shit.

After his father's first press conference as the new general manager of the Colonials.

Forcing his concentration back to where it should be, he

turned to look at his dad, who was smiling like he'd won the lottery. Or the Cup. Which he had, twenty years ago.The fact that his dad was now his team's general manager hadn't quite sunk in yet. Just something else to mess with his head.

As his dad continued to speak to the press, he thought back to the moment his parents had asked him to dinner three months ago. Right before the Redtails had headed into the Calder Cup playoffs.

He remembered the look on his dad's face and immediately thought, "Oh shit, who died?"

His second thought, after his dad had dropped his news, was, "Well, shit, guess I need to find a new team."

His expression must have broadcast his thoughts because his mom had sighed while his dad had shaken his head and leaned on the table.

"Nothing will change for you, Brody. You will always be my son first and my player second. And if this is going to affect our relationship or your game, I won't take the job."

His dad had meant every word. Which meant Brody could either tell his dad not to take his dream job or suck it up and keep an open mind.

He'd chosen the latter, obviously. No fucking way would he be a whiny little shit and tell his dad he was about to ruin Brody's life. Because he wasn't going to ruin Brody's life. Loads of hockey players played for their dads. The sport was inbred all the hell over the place.

But...

"This team has always meant more to me than any other and I'm looking forward to putting together the best group of guys on the ice, which, of course, includes my son, Brody."

Now he couldn't help himself. He looked at her again and saw the shock still on her face, seconds before she dropped her head and started tapping on her phone.

That pretty much sealed the deal for him. She'd had no idea who he was when they'd fucked each other's brains out last night.

And she'd used that mouth on his cock—

"Brody has been an integral part of this organization for the past three years and will continue to be, I hope for the next decade. This kid does not know the meaning of the word 'quit.' When he was sent down to rehab last season with the Redtails, he helped the team win a Calder Cup championship. You can't keep him down and I don't intend to do anything that will impede his growth."

Out of the corner of his eye, he saw his dad turn to look at him at the same time his sister kicked him under the table with that damn shoe again.

Shit. He had words to say here. Something heartfelt and welcoming. Something meant to show the world how much he was looking forward to working with his dad.

Gabby had wanted him to write something down so he wouldn't forget it. And so she could approve it beforehand. He hadn't been afraid to tell her no and his dad had agreed. Whatever he would say should be genuine and not feel rehearsed.

Well, fuck. Now he couldn't think of a goddamn thing except...

"I'm glad to have my dad home. For me, that's what's most important. That he's happy and that my mom's happy."

The chuckle from the crowd eased Brody's nerves a little. He wasn't comfortable up here, had never liked being in front of a crowd, much less being the one in the spotlight.

His sister handled it like a pro, because she was. His brother shone like a star, which he was.

Some people argued that being a major league athlete, he would have to like it a little. Had to crave it.

He always considered it a necessary evil. And even though

he knew every face in the crowd today, he only saw one right now.

And for some reason, that made it a little easier. Which made no sense at all.

She stared up at him, still looking shell-shocked but taking notes in longhand, her hand flying along furiously.

He said a few more words, hopefully the right ones, and when he stopped, she stopped writing a few seconds later and their gazes caught and held again. Until his sister stepped in to continue.

"We're both looking forward to having my dad settled here and at home."

His sister continued on for a minute, saying everything he'd just said but better. Then the team owner began to talk. And Brody leaned back in his chair with an audible sigh and hoped no one was watching him. At least *she* wasn't watching him. She'd turned her attention to the owner and was furiously scribbling on her pad.

"Are you okay?" His sister leaned over, making sure her face was turned away from the crowd of reporters before she spoke. "What's going on?"

"I'm fine. Why? What'd I screw up?"

He could tell from the sound of Gabby's sigh that she'd just rolled her eyes at him.

"Nothing. You did great. We'll talk after."

Great. Just what he wanted. To talk to his sister about why he looked like he'd been cross-checked into the boards.

Luckily, the owner spoke for a good five minutes then Coach spoke again and then the assistant coaches.

Everyone was thrilled to have Duncan Mitchell back in Philly.

Brody hadn't lied. Yeah, it was going to take some adjustment but it wasn't going to kill him to work in the same building as his dad. People did it all the time.

The problem was...how the hell was he going to work with *her*?

———

TARA MANAGED to keep her mind on the job after the initial shock of seeing last night's incredible bed partner on stage and finding out he was a member of the team.

Of course, she wasn't over the shock of discovering he was the new GM's son.

Oh hell. She'd had sex with Brody Mitchell.

"We'll open it up to questions now," Gabrielle Mitchell said. "Go ahead and start us off, Mr. Wallace."

While the other journalists took turns asking questions, Tara's brain seemed to be stuck in neutral. She only had a couple of questions and they were all for one man. And it wasn't the man she was supposed to be interviewing.

Luckily, she continued to take notes. At least her subconscious was working even if the rest of her brain had decided to take a leave of absence.

But now she made a conscious effort to get back in the game and ask her questions. She raised her hand.

"Yes, Ms. Downey." Duncan Mitchell smiled at her and she had a momentary flash of Brody's smile from last night. "Your question."

Swallowing hard, she forced herself to return his smile and ask the questions the *Record*'s Colonials beat reporter had texted her.

"How hands-on do you plan to be with the team? I understand from your previous stint in the AHL, you were involved in the day-to-day operation of the team."

Duncan Mitchell acknowledged her question with a nod. So far, the other questions had been softballs. She probably should've started out with one, too. But her dad had never backed away from a challenge and had taught her never to, as well.

"I have the utmost faith in Coach Angstadt to lead the team on a day-to-day basis. I don't plan to get in his way. Yes, we're going to be working together to shore up what I consider to be some of the team's weak areas, but it will be a collaborative effort."

"And what do you consider to be some of the team's weak areas?"

Mitchell's smile grew, but it didn't appear mocking or demeaning. She'd encountered a lot of that as a female covering male sports. She'd learned to ignore most of it and stand up for herself when she needed to.

Most professional male coaches had gotten better about it in the past few years. Maybe because more women covered sports. Maybe because they were trying to evolve or were at least trying not to wind up the butt of a joke on late night TV for being an asshole.

"Special teams. That's the first order of business. We have a relatively young team. Almost half are under the age of twenty-five and, with the recent retirement of Dickie Duchene, our oldest veteran player is thirty-one. That doesn't mean we don't have the utmost faith in this team to get the job done, it just means we're going to be looking at ways to bring more seasoned leadership into the team."

"So are the rumors true you're going to sign RJ Mitchell?"

Even though she didn't cover hockey, she knew about this particular rumor. Hard to live in Philly and not hear it, especially since word leaked that Mitchell had been in the running for the GM position. Maybe it was just a rumor. Maybe not. If you didn't ask, you didn't know.

Duncan Mitchell's smile never wavered. "I certainly won't say no and I won't rule anything out. I will say we're looking at all options right now, Ms. Downey."

With a nod, he looked away and pointed to another reporter for a question.

And Tara released the breath she hadn't realized she'd been holding.

How much more fucked-up could this day get? Christ, she wasn't sure she wanted an answer to that question.

She managed to keep her mind focused on the job at hand for the rest of the press conference, and after another twenty minutes of questions and answers, it began to wind down and she started planning her escape. Before Brody decided to confront her.

She *so* did not want to deal with him. Seeing him on that stage had been enough of a shock for one day, thank you very much.

If she actually had to talk to him...

As soon as Gabrielle took the mic and said, "Thank you all so much," Tara was out of her seat and headed for the door.

She never reached it.

"Tara! It's so good to see you." Sean Wallace reached out for her hand. "I just talked to your dad last week and he said you'd been hired by the *Record*. Welcome to the club."

"Mr. Wallace." Tara had a genuine smile for the older reporter she'd known since she was a kid. "It's so nice to see you, too. How have you been?"

"I've been good. But you need to call me Sean. We're colleagues now. You know, your dad's so damn proud of you. He hasn't stopped telling people about your new job. I'm sure both your parents are thrilled to have you back in the city."

Yeah, she didn't think years of calling this man Mr. Wallace was going to be changed in a day. "They are. And I'm glad to be back. I missed Philly, believe it or not."

He laughed, nodding. "The city does have its charms, but you know that. You also know the people love their sports. And hate their sports, on any given day. You need anything, have any questions, you let me know."

"I will. Thank you, Mr. Wallace."

Shaking his head, the older sports reporter, who'd been part of her life as long as she could remember, patted her on the shoulder then turned to gather his stuff.

And she had a second to believe she had a straight shot to freedom.

"Ms. Downey?"

Shit, shit, shitballs, fuck.

Covering a sigh and pasting on what she hoped was a genuine smile, Tara turned to face Gabrielle.

"Yes?"

"Do you have a few minutes to spare? My da—" She stopped and her lips twisted in a rueful smile. "Mr. Mitchell would like to say hello."

Tara grinned, despite her careening emotions. "You're gonna be doing that a lot for a while, aren't you?"

Gabrielle nodded, sighing. "Yeah. It's still weird, the whole Dad-General Manager thing, if you know what I mean."

"I do. I interned summers at the *Record* in college. Not in sports, because my dad was the editor at the time. But I never felt right saying 'my dad' to my editor, who was only like ten years old than me and still called my dad Mr. Downey."

Gabrielle laughed. "It certainly is a learning curve. Anyway, the new GM just wants a couple minutes to say hello, even if you're not going to be here regularly. If you don't have time now, we can set up something—"

"No, now's fine." Better to rip off the bandage. "I was hoping to introduce myself."

"Great. Just follow me."

Gabrielle led her through the door to the right of the stage, which was now empty. No Brody—or anyone else—to be seen.

Great. That was great. Hopefully he'd had the good sense to disappear. She didn't spot him anywhere in the hall either, and she breathed a little easier.

While Gabrielle led her through the maze of hallways and up a flight of stairs, they made small talk, designed to put Tara at ease.

She appreciated the gesture. Duncan Mitchell was a Philly sports legend. You couldn't grow up in the city and not know his name, even if you weren't a hockey fan.

He'd played here in the nineties, won two Cups with the team before he'd been traded to the Vancouver team in a move that had enraged fans for decades.

The gossips had said Duncan had butted heads with new ownership over the direction of the team.

Whatever had happened, the Colonials hadn't won a Cup since. Recent social media comments on the paper's articles ranged from calling Mitchell a savior to calling him names the editors had to remove for violating standards.

Philly fans either loved you or hated you. There was no middle ground. If they loved you, you could do no wrong. If they hated you... Well, you could find yourself on the other side of the country.

Which is exactly what she said to Gabrielle as they finally entered an office on the far side of the building.

"Yeah, it's an amazing town to work in. When you're winning." Gabrielle waved Tara into a chair in the otherwise empty room and stopped in the doorway. "When you're not..." She shrugged with a resigned look on her face. "Philly fans have long memories. Give me a second and I'll track down my dad. He should've been here by now. I'm gonna go drag him away from wherever he is. He really does want to talk to you."

Gabrielle disappeared and Tara settled into the surprisingly comfortable chair in front of a big wooden desk covered with what looked like a mountain of papers.

She deliberately kept her gaze off it so she wouldn't be tempted to visually snoop. Which meant she was staring at the door when Brody stepped into the open doorway.

"Uh. Hey."

Her heart took off like a shot and she swallowed and hoped like hell she didn't swallow her tongue. She had a moment of blind panic, followed quickly by a rush of heat.

Yeah, that kind of heat. The "oh my god, I had amazing sex with this man last night and I want to have more right this second" heat that made her gut clench and her cheeks flush bright red.

Of course, she couldn't hide her reaction, which left her flustered and short of breath and wanting to just get up and walk away.

She didn't know what to say to his greeting so she simply sat there and stared at him, probably looking like an idiot.

Sighing, Brody looked over his shoulder before stepping inside and partially closing the door, shaking his head, hands out in front of him like he expected her to attack.

"Look, I know this is awkward as hell, but... I need you to know I had no idea who you were last night. Just...don't freak out, okay?"

"I'm not freaking out." Okay, maybe she was just a little, but he didn't need to know that. "And before you ask, I had no idea who you were either."

He shook his head and rolled his eyes at the same time. "I know. I'm not accusing you of...anything. I just... *Shit.*"

Yeah, that was a pretty accurate sentiment at the moment. Shit.

For a brief moment this morning, when she'd crawled out of his bed, she'd considered leaving her name and number because she'd entertained the idea that maybe, *maybe*, they could see each other again. You know, like an actual date where they made small talk and commiserated about family and got to know each other a little more before they tore each other's clothes off.

Which she totally wanted to do even now, when her thoughts should be so far from tearing off his clothes.

"I can't do this right now." Her voice barely over a hiss, she pointed toward the door. "I have to talk to your *father* in a few seconds. I can*not* do that with you here. You have to leave. Now."

His jaw clenched. "Fine. But we need to talk later."

"No, we don't." Her back teeth ground together and she was pretty sure she made a slight growling noise. "That would be a hugely bad idea."

A faint noise from the outer office shot a bolt of fear through her gut.

"Get out of he—"

The door opened and Duncan Mitchell strode into the room.

"Sorry about that, Ms. Downey. Got tied up in the hall. I see you've already met Brody. Thanks for giving me a few more minutes of your time today."

Pasting a smile on her face, Tara turned to face the man who could make her life a waking nightmare and whose son she'd slept with last night.

"No problem, Mr. Mitchell. I appreciate having the chance to talk to you one on one."

She hoped like hell she wasn't blushing five shades of red. And how embarrassing would it be to pass out here in front of

Duncan Mitchell. With Brody still in the room, she could barely breathe. She wanted to stamp her feet and force him to leave, but his dad would think she was mental. And she certainly couldn't come out and say, "I had sex with your son last night so could you please ask him to leave because he's making me insanely uncomfortable?"

Oh my god, what would Mr. Mitchell think of her? Would he buy her explanation that she hadn't known who Brody was last night? It wasn't like he was a new player. He'd been here for three years. She should have known.

Oh my god, she needed to talk to her editor...

Mr. Mitchell smiled, and this close, she saw the resemblance to Brody in his mouth and his eyes and in the shape of his nose. How the hell had she missed that last night?

Because you hadn't been looking last night.

Now it was written all over Brody's face in bold strokes. And speaking of stroking—

Argh! Stop!

"I know you're not going to be covering the Colonials regularly but I wanted to introduce myself so that when you do happen to find yourself in our arena, you're comfortable."

Yeah, well, that'd been blown to shit last night, now hadn't it?

She smiled, hoping she didn't look like a crazed idiot. "That sounds great."

And it would've been. At any other time. Except now, with Brody here.

Her gaze inadvertently slipped toward him again and Duncan followed her gaze.

"Brody, have you formally met Tara? She's new to the *Record* in just the past couple of months, I believe. You're general assignment, I believe, but you mainly cover baseball and basketball. Like father, like daughter. The Mitchells know a little something about keeping things in the family. I guess the Downeys do, too."

She was impressed Duncan Mitchell had that information in his head. "Yes, sir. My dad taught me a lot."

Brody nodded as he sidled toward the door. "Um, yeah, we just met. Look, I'll talk to you later, Dad. I don't want to intrude."

The elder Mitchell nodded, as if his son hadn't just acted like his ass was on fire and he couldn't get out the room soon enough.

"Sure. We're still on for dinner tonight, though, yes?"

Tara couldn't help herself. Her attention was fully glued to Brody's reaction.

"Absolutely. Looking forward to it."

Oh, the guy was so lying. She had no idea how she knew. She just did.

Brody headed for the door but not before he stopped by her side, his face turned away from his dad's so he couldn't see Brody's expression when he said, "Nice to meet you, Ms. Downey. I'm sure we'll talk again soon."

When he left, she thought she'd be able to breathe again.

Yeah, not so much.

"Ms. Downey?"

With a slight shake of her head, Tara snapped her attention back to Duncan Mitchell.

"Yes, Mr. Mitchell."

And hoped like hell that it stayed there.

FIVE

"Dude, why the hell am I staring at your face in this dump? We still have a month before training camp and I gotta stare at your face every day for nine months."

It was a testament to the fact that Brody hadn't had enough to drink that he understood exactly what Shane Conrad had just said.

He'd asked the Colonials goalie to meet him at the dive bar they'd found last season, when they'd been going through a rough couple of weeks last November, before he'd been sent down to the Redtails.

No one had recognized them the first night he, Shane, and Danny Reid had walked through the door looking to have a few drinks somewhere groupies and fans didn't hang all over them or try to tell them exactly what was wrong with their game.

Danny had mentioned this bar a friend had told him about. Unpretentious neighborhood bar in Fishtown, never crowded, unless the Eagles were playing, and low-key.

It had sounded like heaven to Brody and had lived up to the hype.

Now, the place had become a refuge, a place where he and

his friends didn't have to be "professional athletes" and could simply be themselves.

"So...I met this girl last night."

Shane's eyes widened almost comically, causing Brody to sigh and mentally prepare himself for a rough couple of minutes.

"Is that code for 'I got laid last night'?" Lad Marchenko's tone was completely serious. "Or do I miss something in translation?"

"Nah, you're not missing anything, Heartthrob." Danny shook his head at the former Redtail and newest member of their little group. "Brody totally got laid last night. Are we supposed to pat you on the head and congratulate you or..."

Danny held up his hands, his smile classic smart-ass. The former inner-city Baltimore kid with a wicked right shot and reigning champion of the title "Most Likely to Have His Teeth Knocked Down His Throat" for instigating was a player every opposing team hated but would love to have play for their team.

He and Brody made for an odd couple in terms of friendship until you realized they were the opposite sides of the same coin.

"First of all, fuck you all." Brody gave them all the finger. "And second, it got a hell of a lot more complicated today."

"Pregnancy tests don't work that fast, do they?"

Shane's question made Brody roll his eyes. "No. At least, I don't think they do. That's not the problem."

When Brody paused, Danny knocked on the table.

"You gonna share with the class or do we really not care that you lost your cherry last night?"

Lad choked out a laugh while Shane let his head fall back against the booth and stared at the ceiling.

Brody just shook his head and ignored the taunting. Danny's default was smart-ass, which Brody had once assumed was because the guy used humor to defuse situations where his dark skin could invite insults from less-evolved fans.

But after he'd gotten to know him, Brody realized that was just Danny. Derek Flaherty, Redtails defenseman, reminded Brody of Danny, in some ways. But where Derek's humor was more Three Stooges, Danny's was whip-smart and brutal. He could insult you with a couple of words and you wouldn't realize he'd cut you to the bone until an hour later when you noticed you were bleeding.

"Fuck you. I've got a real problem here."

"Then spit it out. We're waiting with bated breath."

And now that he had their attention, Brody was having major second thoughts. But damn it, he needed some input.

"Okay, look, I can't give you her name but—"

"Wait." Shane shook his head. "What? Why?"

"Do you know her name?"

Lad's follow-up question made Brody's temples throb.

"You know, I think this was a bad idea. Let's just for—"

"No, man," Danny broke in. "Just tell us what the hell happened. We'll sit here and wait until you get your shit together. We'll gag Lad if we have to."

"Your dick is not big enough to—"

"Lad." Shane held a hand in the air. "I swear to God if you complete that sentence I will tape your mouth shut. Brody, just spit it out."

Brody finally unclenched his teeth enough to talk. "Fine. I took a girl back to my place last night. We spent a couple of amazing hours in bed and today I find out she's a sports reporter for the *Record*."

Dead silence for several long seconds.

"And?" Danny looked at him like there needed to be more to the story.

"What the hell do mean, 'and'? Isn't that enough? I can't be screwing around with a local fucking reporter."

"So you didn't know who she was last night?"

Brody shook his head at Shane's question. "I found out at the press conference this morning for my dad."

"I imagine that was awkward."

Danny's dry understatement made Lad laugh. Bastards.

"Ya think?" Brody grimaced. "No fucking shit."

"Did she sleep with you for information?"

Lad's question put Brody's back up at the slight against Tara. "No. She had no idea who I was."

Lad looked skeptical. "And you believe that? Or do you only want to believe?"

Did he?

Don't be a dick.

He shook his head. "If you'd seen her face, you'd believe her, too. She didn't know."

"So then what's the problem?" Danny cocked his head to the side and looked at him with his brows raised. "You had good sex. Move on. Other fish in the sea."

"It was fucking awesome sex."

Shane's eyes rolled so hard Brody figured the guy gave himself a headache. Lad and Danny just laughed.

"I'm happy for you. Seriously. You got laid. Your dick's happy." More wit from Danny. "But, dude, sleeping with a reporter... That will *not* make good pillow talk."

"What is pillow talk?" Lad asked.

Danny took that one. "What you talk about after sex."

With a completely straight face, Lad said, "You talk after sex?"

Shane shook his head, then closed his eyes for several long seconds. "Dude. Have you *ever* dated the same woman twice?"

Lad shrugged. "Why would I do that?"

Brody winced because he would've said the exact same thing two days ago.

Today...

"Fuck."

Danny nodded. "Yeah. You're pretty much fucked. You need to write her off. Sorry, man, but I think it's your best option."

Damn it. He didn't want it to be the best option. He wanted a damn option where he got to see Tara again. Preferably naked and in his bed.

"Dude, I can practically hear you thinking from across the table." Danny's expression held a world of cynicism. "You know I'm always right when it comes to women. Leave this one alone."

Yeah, that was total bullshit. Danny was never right about women. The guy fell in love faster than he could skate. And Danny was one of the fastest skaters in the league. But as fast as he fell in love, he fell out of it just as quickly. The guy was looking for the perfect woman. Wasn't going to happen.

But Brody didn't disabuse the guy of his fantasy. Or ask him how fast it'd taken his last relationship to tank.

He simply nodded and let Danny and Lad turn the conversation to training camp, which started in September.

Ten minutes later, Danny and Lad headed over to the bar to get another round, leaving him and Shane to stare at each other across the table.

Shane wasn't buying his quiet acceptance.

"You really want to see her again?"

Brody took a second to think about his answer. "I honestly— Shit. I know I shouldn't but... yeah. We had a fucking awesome night. And I'm not just talking about the fucking."

"All right, so, look." Shane leaned over the table to make sure Brody could hear him over the music. "I think you should talk to her. Otherwise, you're just never gonna know and it'll eat at you."

"Says the man whose girlfriend is the sweetest woman alive and loves you for some inexplicable reason. How's Bliss like living in Philly?"

Shane's grin widened. The dude was so in love with his girl, it was almost too easy to rag on him. But it'd be like kicking a puppy. They were just so perfect together.

"She's loving it. She got that job she wanted at that bridal shop on Market."

"You make girlfriend work?" Lad shook his head as he slid back into the booth. "I thought that was why women dated professional athletes? So they do not have to work."

Shane sighed but otherwise ignored Lad. And even though Brody tended to side with Lad on this one, he gave Lad an elbow in the side.

Bliss was a sweetheart. Anyone who saw Shane and Bliss together could see how much in love they were. They reminded Brody of his parents, who still loved each other even after thirty-five years, four cross-country moves, and a couple of months where his dad hadn't been sure he'd ever play again.

And nothing like Brody's ex, Angelica, who'd been a straight-up bitch who'd nearly cost him his career when she'd threatened to leak a fake story about Brody when he'd dumped her.

"Tell her congrats from me." Brody grinned. "So...are there gonna be wedding bells next summer?"

Shane's slow grin made Brody's brows rise.

"Wait, did you already ask her?"

Shane shook his head. "Not yet. But I'm going to. So don't make any plans to go out of the country end of next June."

"Hey, man, that's great." And it was. "I'm happy for you. Truly. Bliss is one of a kind."

Shane's grin said everything. "Doesn't mean there isn't a one-of-a-kind girl out there for you. And you'll never find her if you don't take some chances."

"Yeah, but—

"No." Shane cut him off, shaking his head. "Man, if you really like her, life's too short. And you're not gonna play hockey forever. I'd hate to see you pass up a good opportunity that practically fell into your lap."

TARA HEADED INTO THE NEWSROOM, head down, her only goal to get to her desk.

She didn't want to talk to anyone, didn't want anyone to talk to her, and she most certainly did not want anyone to ask why she looked like she needed to breathe into a paper bag for a few minutes.

She'd managed to hold herself together in the taxi on the way back to the office. But as she'd taken the elevator up to the third floor, she felt her lungs begin to work a little harder. Like someone had settled a weight on her chest and it was slowly crushing her.

Which made panic race through her blood like poison.

She had an article to write for tomorrow about the press conference and her short one-on-one with Duncan Mitchell. She had interviews to set up with the Philly MLB rookies, who were heading into their first playoff season. She had notes to transcribe and a Sunday feature to write about a couple of local kids who'd set a world record for hitting home runs.

She had to stop thinking about Brody Mitchell. And last night. And her shock when she'd discovered who he was.

She did *not* want to explain to her friends why she never

wanted to discuss last night again, because if she did, she'd have to explain today's press conference and that was so not—

"Downey, how was the presser?"

Her head popped up at the sound of her name. Sports editor Elliot Fleischer's voice cut through the newsroom like a knife. He was old school, from his button-down shirt to his loosened tie and his perfectly pressed dress pants. The only concession he made to the more casual office dress code was his shoes. Black Converse.

Taking a deep breath in an attempt to get her agitation under control, she changed her trajectory and headed for his office at the back of the sports department.

Might as well get this over with.

"Good. Nothing unexpected, but I did get to talk to Mitchell for a few minutes alone. He seems like a nice guy."

Fleischer nodded and waved her into his tiny office, then sat behind his desk and pulled up something on his monitor. Probably the budget for the next day.

"You've got twenty inches to fill for tomorrow."

Nodding, she mentally calculated how long that would take her to write as Fleischer asked a few more questions about the press conference and she gave him the rundown.

"You hear anything more about the oldest Mitchell kid being signed?"

She swallowed the smart-ass comment on the tip of her tongue about the "Mitchell kid" being nearly thirty years old and just shook her head.

"I asked. He gave the 'We're looking at all options' answer. Complete shutdown."

"All right. What about the other Mitchell kid? He was there, too, right? You talk to him?"

Her cheeks tingled and burned. "Not for the article. I did speak to the sister—"

"Right, right. She's there, too. Anyone give you any shit about your dad?"

The change of subject was abrupt, but she was used to Fleischer's whiplash-inducing conversation by now.

"No. Mitchell had a few nice things to say and Gabrielle practically gushed about how much she admired him. It was nice to hear."

"Yeah, well don't let them butter you up. New GM usually means new system, new controversies. Good news. Anything else?"

"Yes. I need to tell you something."

His gaze narrowed. "Why do I get the feeling I'm not going to like this?"

Because he wasn't. "I just want you to know, I had a previous encounter with Brody Mitchell. At the time, I didn't know who he was. When I realized who he was today, I wanted to tell you before it became a problem."

It took Fleischer several seconds to answer while he stared at her.

"Are you telling me this encounter was...non-professional?"

"If you mean not on company time and personal, then yes."

Fleischer's gaze narrowed down to laser beams. Most of the sports staff believed he could read minds. Truly, they did.

"Can you honestly look me in the eyes and tell me you didn't know who he was and that he never told you his name?"

She held his gaze steady. "Yes, sir. I only found out today. I was...more than a little shocked when I realized who he was."

"And will this be an ongoing thing?"

"Not if it's going to affect my ability to do my job."

Leaning back in his chair, Fleischer stared at her in silence for several long seconds before he sighed hard.

"I can't dictate your personal life, Downey. I appreciate that you 'fessed up as soon as you realized who he was. But if you're planning to see him again, you're not going to be assigned to cover anything Colonials. Not while you're...what? Dating? Do people your age still date? Don't answer that." Shaking his head, Fleischer pursed his mouth like he was sucking lemons. "We hired you to cover baseball and basketball, not hockey. I expect you to know there's going to be no non-professional encountering of any athlete you cover on a regular basis. Are you planning to see the Mitchell kid again?"

Was she? "I..." She blinked then nodded. "I honestly...don't know. Maybe?"

Sighing hard, he rapped his knuckles on the desk. "Can't fault you for being honest. The embargo stands. Write your article about today's presser. I'll go over it with a fine-tooth comb and we'll run it with a by-the-*Record*-staff byline."

"Yes, sir."

His shook his head. "Christ, stop with the 'sir.' I already feel a hundred years old. I need your article by four."

"Yes, si— Yes. Absolutely." She got up to leave. "It'll be done."

Turning, she headed out of his office but heard him mutter, "Encounter, my ass," under his breath before she was out of hearing range.

Slowly dying of mortification, she put her head down and headed for her desk, wrapped herself in the sweater she wore when she wrote, and huddled down into her chair.

Everyone knew if she was wearing her sweater not to bother her unless the building was burning. When she wrote, she shut out the rest of the world through sheer force of will and wouldn't acknowledge you unless you got in her face or smacked her on the back of the head.

Which was exactly what Lindsay did a half hour later.

"Hey, I'm gonna go get something to eat. You wanna come or you want me to bring something back for you?"

With a sigh, Tara figured she should get up and go with Lindsay, at the very least to walk off some of this excess energy. She'd felt it building with every second until she knew she needed to release some of it before she blew.

"I'll come along. I could use some air."

Shedding her sweater and grabbing her wallet from her purse, she followed Lindsay to the elevator, knowing her friend had noticed her agitation and was just waiting until they were alone to interrogate her.

As soon as they were in the elevator with no one else in sight, Lindsay studied her a little more carefully.

"Something happen at the presser?"

"You could say that."

Lindsay's eyes widened. "That doesn't sound good. Someone give you a hard time?"

"I'll explain." Tara made a show of looking around as the doors opened on the ground floor. "Just...let's get out of the building. Okay?"

Lindsay nodded and they didn't speak again until they were on the street and heading toward their favorite deli.

A block away from the building, Lindsay couldn't wait anymore.

"Does this have something to do with what happened last night?"

"He was there."

Lindsay mouth dropped open and she almost tripped over the uneven pavement.

"What?"

Tara grabbed Lindsay's arm and dragged her into the deli, which she'd almost passed.

"You heard me. And it gets better. He's a player."

"What do you mean? He's a—" Lindsay's eyes got so wide, Tara was afraid her friend was going to keel over. "Oh wait. You mean he's a *hockey* player? Like...a Colonials hockey player? You slept with a *Colonials* player?"

"Maybe you could say it a little louder so everyone can hear," Tara muttered under her breath. "Take it down a little, Lins."

"Shit. Sorry."

Lindsay pulled a face and followed Tara into the deli. They didn't say anything while they gave their orders and grabbed drinks out of the cooler, but Tara knew her friend was practically biting her tongue in an effort not to ask more questions.

As soon as they were settled in a booth in the back, fairly deserted this late after lunch, Lindsay leaned across the table, her chest nearly touching her salad bowl.

"Are you seriously saying you didn't know who he was when you went home with him last night?"

"I told you we didn't give names. And he's a hockey player, not a baseball or basketball player. Those I would've known. Besides, he looks nothing like his roster shot. Brody's last picture looks like he spent a year alone on a mountain as a lumberjack. He had a beard and hair down to his shoulders. Last night, he was clean-shaven and his hair is about an inch long."

"Okay, I can see how you could be confused. But...Wait." Lindsay's eyes narrowed as her brain started to make connections. Which made her a damn good cop reporter. Her brain was basically a steel trap. "Why was he at the press conference? I thought it was just to introduce the new GM."

"It was. But the GM's family was there."

It took about a second for Lindsay to make the leap. And then her eyes widened.

"Holy *shit.*"

Tara groaned, her eyes closing as she let her head fall onto her crossed arms on the table.

"You slept with the GM's *son*?"

At least Lindsay had the sense to keep her voice down to a hiss this time.

"I didn't know it was him last night."

"I know, but..." Lindsay shook her head, her expression somewhere between shock and amazement. "Damn, girl, when you decide to get laid, you fuck it up in style."

"I know." Tara lifted her head, groaning as she reached for her bacon cheeseburger. Today definitely called for comfort food.

"Was he surprised to see you? Or did he figure out who you were beforehand?"

"No. He didn't know unless he's a first-rate actor, and no one could be that good."

"Did you talk to him?"

"Yeah, for a few minutes afterward. In his father's office before he came in. Not long. I think we were both too freaked out to even know what we were saying."

Lindsay kept shaking her head, like she couldn't stop. "Well, damn. So what are you going to do now?"

"Nothing." She held up her hand to stop Lindsay's impending question. "And before you ask, yes, I told Fleischer. But I plan to tell Brody we can't do...anything. That it wouldn't work.

"What'd Fleischer say after you told him?"

"I think he wanted to strangle me but didn't want to deal with HR paperwork." She shrugged. "He told me I wouldn't be assigned any more Colonials stories."

"Makes sense. And it shouldn't matter anyway. You'll be busy with basketball between the 76ers and Temple and Villanova." Lindsay's expression perked up. "Maybe you and Brody can give it a shot?"

"I don't know, Lins." The ache in her gut was almost impossible to ignore but that's exactly what she was going to do. "I feel like we've already got too many strikes against us."

Lindsay's expression crinkled in lines of sympathy. "I'm so sorry, hon. You liked him, didn't you?"

Yeah, she did. And damn it, it wasn't fair. Why did this shit always happen to her?

She shook her head. "It doesn't matter. I can't do anything about it now so I'm just going to tell him we can't see each other and then ignore what happened."

Lindsay's eyebrows rose. "Are you going to be able to?"

Truthfully, Tara wasn't sure. But she looked Lindsay in the eyes and lied her ass off.

"Of course."

SIX

Phone in hand Wednesday afternoon, Brody tapped out the number on the card he'd swiped from his sister's desk after the press conference.

He was about to do something incredibly stupid and reckless. And totally out of character.

Okay, maybe not so out of character, at least not the reckless part.

Stupid, he wasn't. Usually. This could be really stupid.

But...he hadn't been able to stop thinking about Tara all last night. He'd fucking dreamed about her. And this morning when he woke, she was his first thought, the only thing on his mind when what he should be thinking about was getting stronger so he'd be ready to play when the season started in October.

His focus needed to be squarely on his conditioning.

At the very least, he needed her to tell him to fuck off. And he would.

And if she didn't?

He'd jump that shark when he came to it.

More like, you'll jump her bones every chance you get.

"Jesus, you're a fucking idiot."

He put the phone down on the table next to the couch then picked it up again seconds later.

"Fuck it."

He tapped the call button.

It rang. And rang. And just before he was about to hang up, he heard an out-of-breath "Hello?"

"Uh, hey, Tara. It's, uh, Brody Mitchell."

He wasn't sure but he thought he heard her suck in a quick breath. And maybe choke on it just a little.

"Brody? What—why are you calling?"

Good question and one he probably shouldn't take offense to. But he did.

"I think we need to talk."

She didn't even pause to think. "I don't think we have anything to talk about. That night was a..."

What? A mistake?

If she really thought that, why didn't she just say it?

"Was what, Tara?"

She fell silent and he all he wanted was for her to talk. The sound of her voice made him hard. That in itself told him he'd been right to call. And the fact that she still hadn't hung up on him gave him hope.

"Look," he said, "I understand where you're coming from but...I really think we need to talk about what happened."

Another pause. And then a huff. "And by talk you mean sex. Or am I wrong?"

Fuck no, she wasn't wrong. All he'd been able to think about today was sex with Tara. He couldn't make himself believe he'd never again have sex with Tara.

"Honestly, no, you're not wrong. Yes, I want to get you in bed again, but I also think we need to discuss...everything that happened."

Her pause this time was longer but he knew she hadn't hung up because the call didn't disconnect.

He hoped she'd done her homework. If she had, she'd know he wasn't going to give up. He had a reputation for patience on the ice. Offense hated him because he couldn't be deked.

And the reason they couldn't was because he spent hours studying his opponents.

Not that she was an opponent. But he figured he had to treat her as one until he got her where he wanted her. Which was in front of him. And under him.

And if they happened to get naked and have sex again, well, that would be a bonus.

"Fine." She sounded as if she were giving in only because she had no other choice but they both knew that wasn't true. Still, he didn't call her on it. "We can meet for coffee. Or something. Or meet in the library or the museum. I'm *not* coming to your place."

Choking back a laugh, he shook his head, although he knew she couldn't see him. "Afraid you won't be able to resist me?"

The second the words were out of his mouth, he wanted to take them back. Smart-ass comments were *not* going to get him what he wanted.

"Wait." He spoke before she could tell him to shove off. "Scratch that. Forget I said it. Look, let's meet at Haven again. I'll reserve a private dining room. We can eat, we can talk. You can throw a glass of champagne in my face and storm out if I do anything you think is over the line."

A couple of heart beats later, she released an audible sigh laced with amusement. "That happen often?"

Her drawl held a challenge, one he definitely wanted to answer.

"Once or twice." Actually, it'd only been once and the

woman in question had nearly destroyed his career. "But I don't think I deserved it."

"Of course you didn't."

That drawl again. A guy could get addicted to that.

"Meet me tonight at seven. At the desk, ask for me and they'll tell you where to go."

He heard her take another audible breath.

"Fine. Tonight at seven."

She didn't sound thrilled but he still wanted to pump his fist in the air in triumph. "You don't have to sound like you're going to a funeral."

"I'm still not sure this is a good idea."

He'd make sure she thought it was a great idea by the end of the night. Hopefully.

You're not really known for your skills with the women, are you?

"I'll see you tonight. And Tara..."

"Yeah?"

"Thanks."

"For what?"

He laughed at the suspicion in her voice.

"For agreeing to meet. I just think we need to talk."

"Sure." A small pause. "But that's all we're doing. Talking."

Not if he had anything to say about it. "I'll see you tonight."

He hung up before she could hear the triumph in his voice. Because he felt like he'd won the fucking lottery.

"YOU'RE GOING to do *what* exactly?"

"You heard me the first time." Tara bit her lip as she contemplated her closet, her phone on speaker on the bedside table. "Don't make me repeat it. Now what the hell should I wear?"

"A dunce cap and a scarlet A on your chest?" Ethan snorted. "Are you insane? This has bad idea written all over it and you're usually not this reckless. I mean, I know we haven't known each other forever but this just doesn't seem like you. What's going on?"

"Nothing's going on. And nothing will go on."

"Then why are you going?"

Good question. "Because I feel like we left some things unsaid. And I need to say them."

"Like what?" Before she could answer, he continued. "Look, I'm not being facetious. I'm seriously interested in what you think you need to say."

So was she. Which was why she'd called Ethan to talk her out of going.

Except...

"I just feel like we need to talk, to get things off my chest so I can stop obsessing. Monday night was so intense and now I just..."

"Just what?" Ethan prompted when the silence dragged on.

"Oh, I just feel like I have things to say and I need to say them to his face." And look at his handsome face. And maybe kiss her way up his— "So what should I wear?"

"You need me to tell you what to wear on a date in a private dining room with a guy you had wild monkey sex with?"

Shit.

With a muted growl, she grabbed her phone off the table and flung herself on her back on the bed. "You're not helping."

"Yes, I am. I really am." Ethan's tone was annoyingly rational. "And you know it. You just don't want to admit it. Hon, you know this is a bad move. I mean, the sex couldn't have been *that* good."

When she didn't answer, because to answer would have

meant admitting something to herself that she hadn't wanted to admit, Ethan released a little snort.

"Are you telling me the sex really was that good? Good enough to possibly tank your ability to do your career?"

"I'm not saying it was the best sex ever in the world." Though for her, it had been. "I'm just saying it was the best sex I've ever had. And..."

"And?"

Ethan's voice held an almost comical amount of trepidation.

"I like him."

Ethan's loud exhale echoed through the phone and now she totally expected him to list all the ways this could blow up in her face again. Maybe this time it would stick. And he was absolutely right. She should be nowhere near Brody.

"Damn it, Tare. That's the one thing I don't have an answer for. Except...wear a skirt so you can pull it up and won't have to take it off altogether."

It took a second for her brain to catch up to what Ethan meant. And when it did, heat flooded her body from head to toe. And every place in between. Some places more than others.

Well, shit. Now she was totally going to wear a skirt.

"Nothing's going to happen." Damn, what a lie that one was. "I just...need to go to show myself that we really can't do this. Does that make sense?"

"In a weird way, yes. I still think you're borrowing trouble."

"You sound like my ancient Aunt Mamie."

"Maybe your Aunt Mamie's smarter than you."

"She's ninety and has dementia but you might be right. I'll let you know tomorrow."

She heard Ethan's "hmph" loud and clear through the phone. "If I don't hear from you sometime tonight, I'm going to know she's got more sense."

"I still don't know what to wear."

"At the very least, wear underwear."

She huffed out a little laugh that didn't have a lot of amusement. "Maybe I should invest in a chastity belt."

"Maybe you should." Ethan almost sounded serious. "Hey, you want me to text you at eight? If you need an out, you can rush to my bedside where I'll be mourning my dead...somebody."

"Sounds good." But she wasn't going to need the excuse because nothing was going to happen.

Then why was she eyeing that slinky black dress near the back of her closet?

"I gotta go."

"Tare? Try not to lose your heart tonight. Okay?"

"I won't." *Ha.* "I'll be fine. It'll be fine. Thanks for listening."

"Uh-huh. You know, if you have sex with the guy again, I'm gonna want details. I have a thing for hockey players, too."

She didn't have a thing for hockey players. She had a thing for *one* hockey player.

"Night, Ethan."

She hung up before he could throw anything else at her and confuse her even more.

With a sigh, she forced herself off the bed, grabbed a dress—not the one in the back, she had some sense left—and pulled it on.

She added a little more makeup than she'd worn last night, simply because the simple flowered swing dress needed it.

Or so she told herself. Earrings, simple necklace...

All the while the little voice in the back of her head was getting louder.

That little voice was laughing at her.

Are you seriously going through with this? What are you really doing?

If she'd been thinking rationally, she never would've told

him yes. She would've written off that one night and forgotten about it.

But...Brody was hard to forget.

Or maybe he was just the first guy in a long time to flick her switches. Maybe, after tonight, she'd be able to write him off as just another guy who didn't live up to the fantasy in her head.

By the time she walked into Haven's lobby and asked for Brody, the laughter was almost deafening.

The brunette behind the counter gave her a bright smile and directed her toward the atrium.

"There's an entrance to the hall to the right then the private dining rooms are to the right. You're looking for number nine."

After she thanked the girl, Tara headed in the right direction but got sidetracked for several long seconds by the beauty of the atrium. The topiaries and colorful garden plots grabbed her attention and wouldn't let go. Whoever had designed this space deserved a damn award.

The entire hotel exuded luxury and, for whatever reason, put her at ease, when she should've been hyperventilating.

Or maybe, dressed as she was, she felt she fit in here tonight. Two nights ago, she'd been here for work, dressed for work, and had felt out of place.

You really shouldn't be here now.

But not because she didn't belong. She'd long ago gotten over the feeling that she was an imposter, simply because she'd been adopted.

No, she shouldn't be here because she might be about to make a really bad career move. There's no way she should be dating an athlete when she covered athletes.

And yet... Her dad was good friends with hundreds of athletes and it had never affected his ability to do his job.

How was that any different?

Ugh.

Shaking her head, she felt her curls brush her neck, revealed by the low back of her dress. Her dress looked tame, in sunny colors that complemented her darker skin, but it clung to every curve and bared more than you noticed at first glance.

It was an invitation to touch. She wanted him to touch her.

She shouldn't want him to touch her. And yet, here she was.

Glancing over her shoulder, she looked to see if she knew anyone milling around the lobby. She didn't. Which was ridiculous. She'd told her editor she might see Brody again. He hadn't fired her or told her she couldn't. She accepted the fact that she wouldn't be covering the Colonials at all and that her career might be hampered by it.

She'd covered her bases and accepted the rules. And when she told Brody she couldn't see him again, everything would be fine. Back to normal.

Yeah, back to being alone.

Shit.

It wasn't hard to convince her feet to move. Her body knew what it wanted and it was in one of the rooms in front of her.

Excitement flooded her body, making her skin tingle and her gut clench. Not to mention her thighs.

From what she could tell, the dining rooms looked out into the atrium. The view would be amazing. Of course, she wasn't sure she'd be looking anywhere other than at Brody.

How the hell had he managed to get under her skin this fast? Yeah, the sex had been good—

No, the sex had been amazing. At least, she could be completely honest about that, even if it did cloud her judgement. And right at this second, she didn't care.

She reached the right door and didn't know whether she should knock or just walk in. Maybe he wasn't even here yet, in which case she'd be standing here staring at the door when he arrived and she'd feel stupid.

Stop stalling. Just open the door.

Pressing the handle, she pushed open the door, took a deep breath, and stepped inside. She'd been right. The view was amazing. Except she wasn't looking at the atrium.

Brody stood in front of the window, looking so damn handsome, her hands clenched into loose fists and her breath caught in her throat.

With his hands in the pockets of blue pants and his white dress shirt unbuttoned at his neck and pulled tight across those broad shoulders, he very nearly made her swoon.

Yes, her friends would laugh at her for using that word but it was the only one that fit her current state.

Staring at him now, she felt a little light-headed. Of course, that could be due to the fact that she hadn't taken a breath in several seconds.

Idiot. Breathe.

"Hi."

The sound of his deep voice intensified the feeling of swoonishness. Was that even a word? Oh hell, did it even matter?

"Hi."

They stood and stared at each other for another few seconds until, finally, he shook his head and moved forward, breaking the spell.

"Come in. Please."

He reached for her right hand, which was already stretching toward him, and tugged her closer, moving her far enough forward that he could close the door behind her. Sealing them into the room and cutting off the rest of the world.

Still holding on to her hand, he looked down into her eyes.

"Thanks for coming."

Her stomach did somersaults at the sound of his deep voice.

She nodded because she couldn't think of a way to respond

that wouldn't reveal just how badly she'd wanted to see him again. Because she really shouldn't want it so much.

Releasing her hand, he took a step back and gestured to the table. "I wasn't sure what you'd want so I didn't order anything yet. Do you want to start with drinks and appetizers?"

Alcohol. Yes, please. "That sounds like a plan. White wine for me."

Hopefully that would get her heart to slow down a little.

Nodding, he turned to pick up the phone on the table by the loveseat near the window.

Of course the private dining room was big enough to hold not only a table for two but a loveseat that faced the window into the atrium.

Trying not to shake her head at the understated luxury, she sank onto the velvet cushions while he gave their order to whoever was on the other end of that line.

Wine for her, beer for him and...nachos.

Her lips quirked in a smile that she quickly controlled.

Such a small thing, but it set her at ease in a way nothing else might have right now.

He was just another guy. Yeah, he might be a professional athlete but he was still just a guy. A guy who'd played her body like he'd known her for years and made her come multiple times. A man whose body she wanted to run her hands all over like she owned him. Which she didn't. Because she couldn't.

When he hung up, he looked down at her and his mouth curved in a grin. Probably in response to hers.

"What's the smile for?" He walked around the loveseat to stand in front of her. "Don't get me wrong. I like it. A lot. I'm just...curious."

Her grin widened. "Nachos?"

His grin vanished under a frown. "Sorry, did you want something—"

"No, no, no." She shook her head. "Nachos are great. I love nachos." She reached for his closest hand, wanting to erase that frown. "I just...wasn't expecting a place like this to have nachos."

The second she touched him, his gaze dropped to their hands. Then his grin returned and his gaze shot back to hers as he tightened his fingers around her hand.

"I could order frog legs, if you want. Or fish eggs. Or snails." He shrugged. "Okay, maybe not the snails. But I'm partial to nachos. And I'm being good. I didn't order the potato skins."

"I'm glad you picked the nachos. That other stuff sounds icky. Maybe save the potato skins for next time."

She realized what she'd said the second it left her mouth but she didn't want to take it back. She wanted a second time.

"Sure." His lips curved in that perfectly lopsided grin of his. "We can do that."

His hand tightened on hers for a second as they continued to stare into each other's eyes. Then, just when it might have gotten awkward, he turned, releasing her as he slid onto the cushion next to her then made a point of staring out into the atrium.

He didn't sit right up against her, but the warmth of his body filled the space between them and seeped into her own. She knew from experience that the guy gave off heat like a furnace.

"I'm not really a garden guy," he stuck his chin toward the window, "but that's really nice."

Her lips curved as he attempted the small talk she knew he hated. "Have you been here before? I mean, in the private dining rooms? I know you've been in the hotel."

He nodded. "Yeah, but not for a while." He looked like he wanted to say something else but decided against it. "I figured you wouldn't want to have this conversation in public so I thought this would work. Since we're just going to talk."

Talk. Right. They needed to talk.

If he'd invited her back to his apartment, things definitely would've gotten awkward. Okay, more awkward. She would've spent most of the night trying not to think about what they'd done on his couch, on his stairs, in his bed...

Here, there was none of that baggage. Just her and him and all the baggage they'd brought with them. She stifled a sigh.

"Talk. Yes." Nodding, she continued to stare at him, though now it was at his profile. "We need to talk."

His nose had been broken at least once, the slight bump near the top an imperfection that only added to his rugged charm. He also had a scar on his forehead that was probably usually hidden because his hair was normally much longer.

"Why did you cut your hair so short?"

His grin became a little cocky as he turned to look at her. "You looked me up, huh?"

Embarrassment rose from her chest and tried to flood her cheeks but she shoved it back.

"I did. Of course, I should've done that last week."

What she kept to herself was the fact that, if she had, they never would've ended up in his bed last night.

Brody chose to ignore that little elephant.

Instead, he lifted a hand to ruffle the short strands. "I figured I should look a little more civilized for all the pictures because of my dad's new job. Probably won't be cutting it anytime soon. What else did you find out about me besides the fact that I cut my hair?"

"That I should've known who you were Monday."

"I'm glad you didn't." Now he looked straight into her eyes. "And don't tell me it was a mistake. Monday night was not a mistake. And even if it was, I'd absolutely make it again."

And there was the intensity she'd fallen for. A rush of adrenaline lit her blood on fire then settled into her stomach in a ball of flame.

Damn him for making her admit, at least to herself, that he wasn't the only one who'd made that same mistake. Again. Sitting here next to him, she knew she would've done the same. He had to know that.

The look in his eyes hinted that he did, but a knock on the door sliced through the building tension and he got up to answer it.

He returned seconds later with a rolling cart holding their drinks and the nachos.

"So, the question," Brody said, as he parked the cart next to the table, "is where we go from here. Because I'm not willing to just walk away."

Hearing him say it made her heart pound again.

It was exactly what she'd wanted to hear. And exactly what she shouldn't want.

Picking up her wine, she took a sip, giving herself a few more seconds to think of a response. And to stop her from sliding her hand into his so she could twine their fingers together again.

"We both know nothing can happen—"

"No, we *both* don't know that." He continued to stand in front of her, staring down into her eyes. "The real question is, how badly do you want see me again?"

Damn him. She shook her head as she transferred her attention once again to the atrium. This situation wasn't fair. Nothing about this was fair.

Frustration roiled in her gut.

"If you did your homework, then you know I only started this job a month ago. I was hired to cover baseball and basketball, but if we date, I won't be able to cover the Colonials. After the press conference yesterday, I had to tell my editor that you and I had a…an encounter before I knew who you were."

"And what'd he say? That we can't date?"

That would've been easier, wouldn't it? "No. But he made it clear that if we have any kind of relationship outside of work, I'll never cover the Colonials."

"And is that a bad thing?"

She wanted to growl in frustration. "No, because hockey isn't my focus. I know how it's played but it's not my specialty. But if people find out you're dating a reporter, they'll think 'So what?' If people find out *I'm* dating an athlete, no matter what sport, they'll question everything."

He didn't say anything for several seconds, and she sat there staring out into the atrium, practically grinding her back teeth into dust. Damn him for making her want to reach for him again, to wrap her arms around his neck and press their bodies together. It wasn't fucking fair.

Then he sat beside her and she swallowed hard as her desire for him flooded her every cell. She'd been so damn foolish to think she could have dinner with this man and not want to jump his bones.

"So what if we don't date?"

Her head whipped around to stare at him as her brain tried to sort out his meaning. Questions crowded the tip of her tongue but he continued before she could let them spill out.

"Hear me out." He lifted his right hand, as if he was being sworn in for jury duty. "Just suspend your disbelief for a few minutes. We're both gonna be super-busy in the next few months. So what if we don't date? If we both have a free night, we can get together. If we want to. If not, no harm, no foul. No strings."

She considered what he was saying carefully for several

seconds, working through her response. But really, all she could say was, "You want to be friends with benefits?"

Otherwise known as fuck buddies. She should've known—

He shook his head. "Why don't we work on the 'friends' part first?"

Friends? Really?

It would never work. No matter how earnest he sounded. How determined. But the fact remained that in the morning, she'd still be working for the paper and he'd be on the ice for the Colonials.

And yet... She wanted what he was selling. She shouldn't, but...

"Tara." His jaw clenched, the muscle near his ear jumping, and she knew he was biting back what he really wanted to say. "Why don't we eat and then we can—"

"I think...I'd like to hear more."

BRODY WANTED to pump his fist in the air and declare victory even though Tara hadn't agreed to anything.

Yet.

He'd walked into this room tonight not really sure what the hell he was going to say when she showed up. *If* she showed up.

Frankly, he'd been surprised when she had.

When she'd opened the door, he'd realized he'd been sure of one thing.

He wanted to see her again.

And now, he knew he'd do whatever it took to make sure this was only the first night of many they'd spend together.

No, he couldn't argue with anything she'd said. There was no way in hell they should consider starting any kind of relationship. It was exactly what he'd been thinking before she arrived.

Then she'd walked through the door and his brain and body had been in total agreement.

He wanted her. However much she was willing to give him, he'd take. And then he'd work on getting her to trust him enough to give him more.

"I propose getting to know one another. Monday night was intense but we both agree it was amazing. I think we'd be fools to ignore that and let it pass us by."

Since he was watching her every move, he could tell he'd hit a nerve. Especially since she didn't deny anything he'd just said.

If he were being honest, he'd admit what he wanted to do right now was kiss her until she agreed to come back to his apartment again. Which was stupid because if he did, she'd probably walk out and not look back. Instead, she was still listening.

But she proved how smart she was with her next words. "You don't have a clue, do you? About just being friends?"

A challenge. He didn't think she realized she'd just thrown one down and he couldn't resist. He was used to thinking on his feet. On the ice, the game could turn on a dime. You either kept up or you sat on the bench. He hadn't made it to the NHL solely on the basis of his family legacy. He'd had to work twice as hard to make it to where he was today.

He *would* make this work. Because for the first time in a long time, he'd met a woman worth the trouble.

"Give me a chance to show you I do."

She went silent again, those pretty eyes practically dissecting him.

"I have a lot more to lose than you do if this doesn't work out."

He couldn't argue that point. He also knew she hadn't walked out yet. Now he just needed to come up with a plan.

"Tell me why I should jeopardize everything I've worked for...for you?"

"Because that night was more than just sex."

At least, it had been for him. He'd never met a woman who incited the response Tara did. Not even Angelica, and he'd briefly considered marrying her.

Tara didn't say anything right away but he could tell she was crafting a response. She was a reporter. She was used to analyzing a situation, asking questions, and getting answers. And if he didn't give her the right answers, she'd write him off.

She hadn't left yet, so he took that as a good sign.

"We only just met. How could it be?"

Reaching for her hand, he wove their fingers together. Her breath caught with a barely audible hitch when they touched and he bit back a smile. She'd felt that same spark he had.

"Chemistry. Connection. Whatever you want to call it. We've got it. I want to explore it. Something like this doesn't happen all the time. At least, not to me."

Her lips pursed, as if she were trying to hold back whatever she wanted to say. He knew enough about her by now to know that wasn't going to happen. She proved him right a second later.

"Chemistry doesn't always translate into relationship."

He knew that. Had firsthand knowledge. And maybe that should've made him take a step back and slow the hell down. But Tara wasn't Angelica. Not even close.

He'd made one hell of a huge mistake thinking Angelica had been more than a fling. And when she'd burned him, threatening to ruin him by spreading lies, he'd cursed himself for months. His friends had thought he'd been depressed about the breakup. He hadn't been. He'd been pissed at himself for not seeing Angelica for who she really was.

Unless Tara was a world-class actress, she hadn't been bull-shitting him.

"But chemistry like the kind we had isn't something to toss aside either. We're both old enough to know that."

Humor flashed across her expression and her lips curved. "Are you trying to tell me I'm old?"

His gaze dropped to study her lips before rising again to her eyes. "No. I'm trying to tell you I'm so fucking hot for you, I might spontaneously combust."

The stunned wonder on her face was worth the truth of his words, no matter how hard they'd been for him to say.

"I'm willing to take this friendship, relationship, whatever you want to call it, as slow or as fast as you want," he continued. "I just don't want you to mistake my restraint for disinterest."

After a long moment, she shook her head, but he was pretty sure she wasn't turning him down. Her next words confirmed that.

"You called yourself feral last night." Her gaze bored into his. "Most people don't see the intelligence behind that snarl, do they?"

He got off on the fact that she didn't let him off the hook easily.

"No. And I'm good with that. But I'm not stupid enough to give up seeing where this thing between us goes."

Another short pause before she huffed out a sigh. "Does anyone ever win an argument with you, or do you grind them into submission with logic?"

Now he grinned and her gaze dropped to his mouth for several seconds. His cock responded with a rush of blood. So far tonight, he'd been able to keep his horniness under control. He needed to continue that if he was going to prove to her that they could do this.

Whatever "this" was. Dating. Sex. Relationship. Friendship.

"I don't get into a lot of arguments with people. Usually not worth my time or the trouble."

Her head tilted to the side. "So you think I'm worth both?"

Hell yes. "Yeah, I do. I think Monday night proved it."

She stared into his eyes again before letting her gaze slip away, back to the glass wall between them and the atrium. He couldn't read her, had no idea what she was thinking.

Then she sucked in a short, sharp breath and shook her head, as if she were trying to shake out the cobwebs.

"Training camp starts in a month."

It wasn't what he'd been expecting her to say, but at least she hadn't gotten up and walked out. So he'd let her steer the conversation wherever she wanted.

"Yeah."

Another short silence while she took a sip of her wine and leaned over to reach for the nachos.

"Are you ready?"

He released a silent sigh of relief, and their discussion turned toward the game while they picked at the nachos then ordered dinner. They both ordered steaks and salads and he put in an order for the dessert sampler, and watched her eyes light up. He had a sweet tooth. Apparently, she did too.

Good to know.

He remained on his best behavior as they ate dinner. Like Monday night, he found it easy to talk to her, easy to find topics that engaged them both.

By the time they started dessert, he was feeling pretty cocky.

Taking the cheesecake off the cart, he picked up a forkful and extended it toward her.

She looked at it, then looked at him.

"They have the best cheesecake in Philly here."

She looked at his fork again before picking up another one and getting her own bite.

He grinned...until she closed her lips around the tines then pulled them out, her lips pursing in a way that made every muscle in his body tighten.

He pulled back the fork he was holding and set it on the table because he was pretty sure he would've choked if he'd taken his own bite. Every nerve in his body went on high alert and the blood rushing through his veins burned like lava.

Holy fuck.

Closing her eyes, she savored the bite of cheesecake with a little hum, which he was pretty sure she'd done just to drive him insane.

When her eyes opened again, they held a hint of a challenge.

"You're right. This is amazing. Aren't you going to have any?"

Tease.

Hell yes, he wanted some. He just didn't want the cake.

Was she just fucking with his head? Taunting him?

Her next words blew that theory.

"I like you, Brody."

Triumph blazed in his gut. "Then say yes."

She held his gaze. "And if I do, then what?"

They'd moved to the table to eat dinner and now he rose to his feet and came around to her side. She watched his every step, watched as he leaned down, put his hands under her arms and lifted her against him.

He'd told himself he wasn't going to push. But the simple act of her taking that bite of cake had pushed him over an edge he hadn't been aware he'd been so close to.

She came willingly, her hands settling on his shoulders, reminding him how she'd used those hands on his body two nights ago.

"Then we can do this."

Fuck easy. If he was going to get her to agree to see him again, it wasn't going to be because he asked her nicely.

No, he needed to show her what she was going to miss if she said no.

Sealing his mouth against hers, he kissed her like he'd been dying to do since she'd walked through the door. Hot and hard and holding nothing back.

At first, she froze, her fingers digging into his shoulders like she was going to push him away.

But he didn't stop. He kissed her with every shred of knowledge he'd gleaned from the other night. He kissed her until their lips were smashed together and stabbed his tongue into her mouth to torment hers.

Drawing every last ounce of sweetness from her mouth, he pressed his erection against her lower belly, showing her how much she affected him. Needing her to know what she did to him.

Finally, after several long seconds, her fingers slid up his shoulders and into his hair, trying to wind around the short strands to hold him in place.

Yes.

With her feet dangling inches off the floor, he carried her to the loveseat and eased down into it. Her knees landed on the outside of his thighs and her hands tugged his head back until she leaned over him. She'd taken over the kiss and he let her. At least for now.

Only seconds later though, she pulled back. Afraid she might try to get away, he put his hands on her hips and held her in place.

"You don't play fair." She tugged on his hair, the sharp pain fleeting. Arousing.

"Yes, I do. I just know how far to push the rules without breaking them."

She stared at him as if trying to pick apart his brain. But she didn't move away and he took that as another win.

She shook her head. "I can't believe I'm even considering this. I'm not normally this reckless."

"That's because you hadn't met me."

After a few seconds, she sucked in a breath and released it on a sharp sigh. Her expression held a mixture of hope and worry.

"I don't want to regret meeting you, Brody."

Her voice saying his name did something to his guts that he'd never felt before. Which was why he'd made the decision to fight for her.

She wasn't wrong. Not about anything she'd said tonight.

But that didn't mean they had to throw up their hands in defeat. They could fight for what they wanted. They just had to be smart about how they did it.

"Then don't. No one needs to know what's going on. When we're together, it's just the two of us. No shop talk."

"Just sex."

He couldn't tell whether that was a question or a demand. So he answered how he thought she'd meant it.

"Just us doing what we want and getting to know one another."

She fell silent then, staring into his eyes, weighing her options.

"Just us. No one else needs to know."

Then she sealed her mouth over his and kissed him until he couldn't breathe.

SEVEN

"Hey, you wanna go out tonight? A couple of us are gonna hit that new place in Manayunk."

Tara didn't bother to look up from her screen late Monday afternoon. "Mmm...maybe?"

Reading through her baseball playoffs preview for Sunday's pages, she thought she had a damn good article.

Over the past two days, she'd gotten a lot of good material for her article. Most of the guys were articulate and knew exactly how to respond to her questions. A few actually had unique answers, or at least answers that hadn't been coached by their PR rep or their agent.

The others, particularly the twenty-year-old rookies who looked like they should still be in high school, had made her feel like she was pulling teeth. Luckily, the team's PR guy had been there to help them along, to draw out more than one-word answers to every question.

"Wait." Ethan rolled his chair next to hers and bumped his shoulder into hers. "Let me rephrase that. You *are* coming out with us tonight and we're going to that new place in Manayunk.

I know there's no game and I know you have off the next couple of days."

She spared Ethan a few seconds for an eyeroll before she sighed dramatically and let her head fall back, eyes closed, as she stretched her legs, knocking over the low heels she'd worn to work this morning and had kicked off earlier to replace with the Eeyore slippers she kept under her desk.

"I've got to finish this article."

"Looks finished to me."

He had her there. She'd been about to send it off to Fleischer when Ethan had rolled over.

"My sisters said something about getting together for dinner."

"So come out after."

It was on the tip of Tara's tongue to say no but just as she was about to make another excuse, Ethan shook his head.

"Please. Tare. I know it's the end of the season but you totally need to blow off some steam. So unless you have a death in the family or you're going to admit you've got some kinky secret affair going on, you're coming out tonight. And," he drew the word out to at least four syllables, "if you do have something kinky going on, you can come out and give me details before you go out. Because there has been *nothing* going on in my life and I totally want to live vicariously through you."

Tara rolled her eyes at Ethan's lame attempt at humor but hid a wince at how close he came to hitting on the truth.

She wanted to talk to someone about Brody and she knew Ethan wouldn't judge. Hell, he might actually be excited for her. It was also true that it was the end of the season and the Phillies had only three days without games this month. That meant that she and the other Phillies beat reporter rarely had down time.

It also meant she hadn't seen Brody since last Wednesday's

dinner at Haven. Her need for him was a steady drip of acid into her bloodstream. She was hoping to see him tonight but he hadn't returned her earlier text yet.

Why are you waiting for a guy to get back to you? Spend the night with your friend.

"If you had let me answer," she finished typing out her last thought before turning to face him, "I would've said okay. Text me the address and the time and I'll meet you there."

"Well, damn. Color me shocked and amazed." Ethan reached over to put the back of his hand against her forehead. "You don't feel like you have a fever."

Rolling her eyes, she shoved his hand away. "There's nothing wrong with me."

Ethan's expression held definite disbelief. "At least nothing a little alcoholic R and R won't fix. I know this month is going to be crazy busy for you and I won't get to see you much so we need to get together when we can."

True. Her schedule would mainly be nights while Ethan's would stay days. She'd also be traveling to some of the games and would be away for days.

"You'll be at some of the games, though, right?" she asked. "Don't you go with a friend who has season tickets?"

"I do. But it won't be the same. I'll be a baseball widow."

His dramatic flourish at the end made her laugh, as it was supposed to, but it also made her realize that she wouldn't be seeing much of Brody, either. The Phillies had only three days off in August. And five in September. And if they made the playoffs, which was pretty much assured since they were having a good season, they'd be playing into October. Brody would be in training camp by the second week of September before his season started in October.

Basketball started in November.

As Ethan rolled back to his desk, she swiveled back around

to face her monitor but her thoughts were scrambled now with the realization that her relationship with Brody didn't have a chance in hell of working.

Seconds later, her phone pinged with a text and she picked it up, grateful for any distraction.

Meet me tonight.

Brody.

She swore her heart skipped a literal beat. Damn him.

They'd texted over the weekend but hadn't been able to connect. Honestly, she'd been a little— Okay, fine, she'd been more than a little disappointed. Which was ridiculous. They'd agreed to be casual about their...affair.

And she'd told herself she wasn't just going to drop her life and run when he beckoned.

I have plans. With a friend.

Why the hell had she added that last bit? She didn't owe him an explanation for anything.

Damn it. Who was she kidding? She really wanted to see him.

Come by after.

The need that hit her almost took her breath away. She wanted to see him. Wanted that more than anything.

Don't you start conditioning training tomorrow? Shouldn't you be resting?

She nibbled her bottom lip while she waited for his response. Even though she already knew the answer.

How old do you think I am?

It took her a second to realize he was making a joke. Then she started to smile and couldn't stop. Such a little thing but knowing she'd gotten him to lighten up felt like a victory.

Old enough to know better.

Old enough to know what I want. And exactly how much rest I need. Pretty sure I can spend tonight and tomorrow night

making you come multiple times. I can sleep tomorrow night.
You're gonna be in D.C. for the games, right?

Holy crap. Lust jolted through her body like an electric
shock. Her thighs clenched and heat shot through her veins.

How the hell did he do that? No other man she'd ever met
had ever made her feel like this.

Why did it have to be him?

She was trying to think of the right thing to say when he
sent another text.

I'm willing to tempt fate if you are.

Damn him. Yes, that's exactly what this felt like. Tempting
fate.

I thought hockey players were superstitious. Do you really
want to anger the hockey gods before the season even starts?

She attempted to bring a little levity back to the conversation but apparently he wasn't having it.

I think spending time with you is a good idea.

Her breath caught in her throat and her heart gave a little
flip. She hadn't known Brody long and she wasn't sure she knew
him well. But that text was one of the reasons she had a hard
time saying no to him.

Even though it was a really bad idea to say yes.

So just say no.

Problem was, she didn't want to say no. Because she knew
eventually this would end. They'd work this hot rush of
hormones out of their systems and they'd move on. And no one
would know what they'd done.

What time?

She had no freaking willpower when it came to this man.

Eleven?

Ethan wouldn't be suspicious if she left by 10:45 tonight,
right? She'd plead a headache.

Okay. See you then.

"Tara. Earth to Tara?"

Ethan's voice dragged her back to the newsroom. And the look on her friend's face promised a whole host of questions she knew she couldn't answer.

"Yeah? What's up?"

Ethan's narrowed gaze "Apparently something that has to do with the text you just got. Hon, is there something going on you want to discuss? Something *I* want to discuss? Because whatever you're thinking about, it's making you hot and bothered."

Her already flushed cheeks burned a little brighter and Ethan's gaze narrowed. He might work in Lifestyle now, but he'd come from City, where he'd covered city council for a year. The guy had bloodhound instincts. He knew she had something to hide.

She didn't want to lie to Ethan but she couldn't tell him what was going on. Not that she thought he would say anything to anyone but because if she told him, she'd want to tell Lins. And she couldn't tell anyone.

"I can't. It's just...something I can't talk about now."

Ethan's gaze narrowed even more. "Are you in trouble?"

She shook her head, her mouth curling in a small grin. "No, it's nothing like that."

He stared at her for a few silent seconds. "Well, I hope you know if you were, you could tell me. My lips would be sealed."

"I know. And thanks. So, you gonna be at the game this weekend?"

As a segue, it was choppy, but Ethan let her get away with it.

"Sure. I'll be there. I'm going with Doug and Josh. Stop by and say hi, okay? I know they'd love to see you again. They ask about you all the time."

Nodding, she agreed to stop by their regular seats. Doug and Josh were huge baseball fans. The fifty-ish couple had been good friends with Ethan's parents and had taken Ethan in when his parents had moved to Florida several years ago while Ethan was still in college at Temple.

"They just want to pick my brain for gossip." She was only partly kidding. Doug and Josh were true baseball fans and lived for any tidbits of information she could give them.

"Of course they will. But they really *do* like you. Almost as much as I do."

"Aw, I love you too."

Ethan's eyes rolled. "Yeah, yeah. Don't think I can't see through you. I know there's something going on with you. I'll get you to tell me eventually."

He was probably right. She just hoped it wasn't after she and Brody went down in flames.

***

"EARTH TO BRODY. Hey, you coming to dinner tonight or you gonna break our mother's heart?"

Tossing his phone onto the couch next to him in his sister's office, he sighed, nodding his head as he did.

"Of course. It's a command performance." He held up his hand before Gabby could say what he knew she was about to. "And before you blast me, you know I would never say that to Mom. Of course I'll be there."

When Gabby rolled her eyes and huffed, he had the childish urge to pump his fist in the air and declare victory. But that's all it was. A childish urge.

Didn't mean it wasn't true.

"Hey, brat."

Gabby's soft-spoken childhood nickname made him stop and pay attention. Really look at her. He realized he had her full attention and that was never a good thing. It made him want to run in the opposite direction.

"Are you really gonna be okay if RJ comes here to play?"

Shit. Shaking his head and sighing, he leaned back in the chair and let his head fall back against the cushion.

"Are we really gonna play this game, Gabs? I thought at least you wouldn't try to blow smoke up my ass. I'm not completely clueless. RJ'll be here by the beginning of training camp. When has Dad ever *not* gotten his way?"

Gabby grimaced as she settled back into her chair across the desk from him.

"You're right. I'm sorry. I don't— It's just— Shit. Dad wants this so badly. He wants both of his sons to play for his team. And he wants everyone on board with it, no matter what. But this is me. You can tell me how you're really feeling."

No, he really couldn't.

And he really needed to get out of here.

He'd stopped by the arena today because his dad had wanted to talk to him. Brody had figured his dad was going to tell him they'd finally signed RJ. Turned out his dad had wanted to discuss having Brody at a few upcoming meetings with ownership.

Afterward, he'd stepped into Gabby's empty office to take a phone call from his agent, who'd called when Brody had been walking through the halls to the parking lot. She'd still been talking to their dad.

When he'd gotten off the phone, he figured what the hell, he'd text Tara. Just to talk.

Which was total bullshit. He wanted to see her. And when he'd gotten her to agree to come over tonight, he felt like he'd won the damn lottery.

But he had to be careful not to look too happy. People assumed grumpy was his normal state of being. If Gabby caught wind of his decent mood, there'd be more questions that he didn't want to answer.

But the fact that RJ would be here in a couple of weeks and the press would be all over his ass...

He just wanted to play the damn game. Not worry about what the hell he was going to say to the press about his brother.

The only member of the press he wanted to talk to was Tara. And not about hockey.

"Gabs." He gave her the look, the one that usually got her to mind her own damn business. "I'm fine. And if I wasn't, you'd know."

She didn't back off this time. Either he hadn't put enough "back the hell off" into his voice or she could tell something was going on. He was afraid it was the latter.

"What's up with you?" She leaned forward, leaning her arms on her desk and staring him down. "You've been...different since you came back from Reading. You actually look happy. I mean, damn, you almost smiled a few times."

He knew she was busting his ass and he was ready to do the same to her but she continued before he could say anything.

"And I know you weren't happy before you got injured."

He considered shutting Gabby down by telling her to mind her own damn business and walking out. It's exactly what he'd normally do.

Yes, she was family and he loved her, but she wasn't entitled to meddle in every aspect of his life. But if he did that, it'd only fuel her curiosity. Still, he didn't want to talk about any of this right now.

He wanted to talk to Tara. And he would. Later. Maybe.

Damn it.

When he didn't answer, Gabby's expression twisted in a grimace.

"Just answer me this," she finally said with a huff. "Does it have anything to do with RJ? Or Dad? Because if it does, we need to talk about it. All of us. We need—"

"Gabs." He shook his head, sighing hard. "It's not RJ. And it's not Dad. Seriously, just...let it go. I'll figure it out and everything will be fine. But don't treat me like an idiot. I fucking hate being kept out of the loop."

Gabby had the grace to look uneasy but then she nodded. "I get it. I do. But Dad and I didn't want to put you in the position where you had to lie. I can't believe reporters haven't been hounding you for comment. Dad and Jim have been in negotiations on this for almost a month."

Jim was RJ's agent. And Gabby wasn't wrong. Not one reporter had mentioned anything since the first few stories about their dad taking over the job although there'd been a few mentions on the NHL Network.

"I guess everyone just figures it's gonna happen." He shrugged. "Don't look a gift horse in the mouth. With the *Record*'s beat reporter on medical leave, breathe easy for a few weeks. It'll get crazy enough in a few weeks."

He and Tara had been really careful about not discussing hockey. It hadn't come up at all during dinner at Haven. Of course, they'd had more important things—

"And you're gone again." Gabby's voice broke through his fog just as his phone began to ring. "What's going on with you?"

Pulling out his phone, he took a look at the screen, realized who was calling, and swiped to answer the call.

"Gotta take this, Gabs. I'll see you at Mom and Dad's."

"Brody—"

"Hey, Shane. Can you hang on a sec?"

He waited to hear Shane's quiet "Sure" before he turned back to his sister with an expectant look.

She sighed, shaking her head. "Dinner tonight. We'll talk then."

"I thought we just got done talking."

Now she gave him the look, the one he recognized from twenty-five years of being the youngest.

He refrained from rolling his eyes. "Text me the time for dinner. I gotta take this."

Gabby looked like she was ready to say more as he made a quick exit, waiting until he was in the hall to talk to Shane.

"Hey. Sorry about that. What's up?"

"Bad time?"

Yeah, actually, it was. His perfect older brother was about to sign with the Colonials and every move Brody made would be judged against him. And Brody was having a secret affair with a woman who made him fucking crazy with lust, a woman whose job was digging up information, like the story about his brother, and sharing it with the world.

"Nah. Just talking to my sister. What's up?"

"Couple of the guys are getting together tonight at my place. You wanna come over?

"Can't. Dinner with my parents. Mandatory performance."

"Come over after. We'll be there for a while."

"Not sure what time we're gonna be done."

"Just show up whenever. We'll be there." A pause. "Unless you got plans."

Fuck. He fucking hated lying to his friend.

"Just not sure I'll be up for anything after I'm done with the family."

Another pause. "Something going on? Everything okay?"

Brody bit back his immediate, sarcastic response. *No, everything's not okay.* Shane didn't deserve to have his head bitten off for being a decent guy.

"Nah. Nothing's wrong. Just...family stuff."

As excuses went, it was weak. But it was also the closest to the truth he could come.

"You know if you need to talk..."

Shane didn't finish his sentence. He didn't need to.

He and Shane had become close friends before Brody had been sent down to the Redtails, which was where Shane had been before being pulled up last season.

If Brody was going to tell anyone about Tara, it would be Shane.

But he couldn't. It just wasn't going to happen.

However, Brody was fairly sure Shane wasn't trying to get him to talk about his love life.

No, Shane was tiptoeing around RJ.

"I'm good, man."

"All right. Just...come over tonight. Unwind."

"I'll let you know later. Thanks for the invite."

One he wouldn't be accepting unless his night went totally to shit.

AS THE ELEVATOR doors closed behind her after depositing her on Brody's floor, Tara paused for a second to take a deep breath.

She'd had a couple—okay, maybe she'd had more than a couple of drinks with Ethan at the bar. She certainly wasn't drunk but she was feeling no pain. Yes, she'd had some food but not enough to harsh the nice little buzz.

On the Uber ride over here, she'd tried not to let her brain get tied up in knots but she couldn't help thinking about the call she'd taken before leaving work to meet Ethan.

With the Colonials beat reporter on medical leave, she'd talked to a sports agent in Los Angeles, one she'd known during her days on the west coast and whom she'd contacted before she'd started seeing Brody.

Off the record, the agent had told her RJ Mitchell's agent was crossing the final Ts on RJ's contract with the Colonials.

After she'd hung up, she'd given herself a couple of seconds to process, then she'd written up her notes from her conversation and sent them to her editor, who'd thanked her for the info. And that had been that.

If she weren't seeing Brody, she would've been all over this story. Now, it'd be assigned to one of the other general assignment reporters...one who wasn't having a relationship with RJ Mitchell's brother.

RJ would be in Philadelphia by training camp. No hardcore Colonials fan would be surprised. The only shock was who the Colonials had to give up for him. That was going to ruffle more than a few feathers and would make for a couple weeks of controversy when it hit the fan base.

Whoever Fleischer assigned the story to would talk to Duncan Mitchell, talk to RJ...talk to Brody. No one would be able to say she'd gotten the information because she was screwing Brody.

Stopping in the middle of the hall, she huffed out a sigh.

Is this really worth it? Is he *worth it?*

She should leave. Now. Before she knocked on his door.

She couldn't make herself do it. She couldn't make her body turn and head back to the elevator.

She didn't *want* to leave.

Why? What was it about Brody that made her reckless enough to hobble her career?

Sure, the man was easy on the eyes but she'd never dated a man strictly because of his looks. She'd learned the hard way that was guaran-damn-teed to end in frustration and the need to smack someone.

The damn man had snuck in under her defenses and now she couldn't stop thinking about him. Maybe because he'd been the first man to put in the time and effort in a very long time.

Getting her feet moving again, she walked to his door and raised her hand to knock, but the door opened before she could.

She hadn't been expecting it and she hitched in a quick breath, her gaze immediately going to his face.

"Hey."

Her eyes narrowed at that short, gruff greeting. Something was wrong. She could hear it in the tone of his voice even though his expression was as close to smiling as he usually got.

"Hey." She walked by him when he waved her in. "Is every-thing okay?"

Closing the door behind her, he leaned against it, crossing his arms over his chest and bending a knee to brace one bare foot against wood.

Her mouth dried and every thought fled her brain. In worn jeans and a tight Henley that showed every muscle in his chest in bold relief, he was every woman's wet dream.

Even with that slightly grumpy look on his face, he was still the most handsome man she'd ever seen. Grumpy looked good on him.

So not fair.

"Yeah," he nodded, "it's definitely better now that you're here."

Oh my freaking god. When the hell had he gone from feral to adorable?

Her entire body wanted to melt into a puddle of goo at his feet. She wanted to throw herself at him, wrap her arms around him, and kiss him until he took her to the floor and they had wild monkey sex right here in front of the door.

Every doubt about why she was here dissipated like steam from a boiling pot.

It's just sex. It's just sex. It's just sex.

Maybe if she kept telling herself that, it would make it true.

"You shouldn't say things like that."

"Why?" He looked genuinely confused for a second before shrugging off her concern. "It's true."

"I'm not questioning your motives. You just make it hard for me to—"

She'd almost said "keep my distance."

But that wasn't what she wanted and she couldn't make herself say the words. No, she wanted the exact opposite. She just couldn't tell him that either.

"Hard for you to what?"

His expression didn't change but she could tell he'd become more wary. Waiting for her to tell him... What? That they were through?

"Hard for me to stay away."

That was just as much the truth as anything else she could have said. But this time his mouth curved in a slight grin.

And oh my god, the man got even hotter.

Heat flooded her body from her toes to her scalp and everywhere in between.

Shaking her head, she just stood there and stared at him while his smile got just a little more wicked.

Pushing away from the door, he walked over to her, settled his hands on her shoulders, and pulled her closer until only centimeters separated them.

"Why would you want to stay away?"

The heat of his body seeped into her skin, making her blood chug through her veins like lava. Her thighs clenched when he leaned closer and her lips parted, expecting his kiss.

Her breath caught in her throat when he rubbed his nose against hers, the caress endearing and sweet and sexy all at the same time.

With her head tilted back as far as it could go, she rose onto her toes, her hands gripping tight to his waist, and nipped at his chin.

"Because you're fucking with my head."

"Back at you." His gaze dropped to her mouth for a split second before coming back to hers. "I'm gonna ask you to use those teeth somewhere else a little later."

She shivered as the electric shock of his voice made her skin tingle.

"You'll have to ask really nicely."

Still smiling, he ran the tip of his nose against her cheek then used his own teeth to nip at her ear.

"I thought you liked me when I'm bad."

The truth was she liked him all the time. The guy would have to do something completely asinine to make her not like him. And that was just something else she needed to keep to herself.

"I like when you use your mouth to do something other than talk."

Sex. Keep it on sex.

That's what they did best.

"Then you're in luck because I'm really not in the mood to talk."

So something had happened earlier.

She had a split second to think about that before his mouth descended and wiped away all rational thought and replaced it with his taste and his touch and...everything he was.

His arms wrapped around her shoulders and dragged her tight against him, trapping her arms between them for a few seconds before she got them loose and wound them around his neck.

As always, she was struck by their height difference, by the way he loomed over her and by how much she liked it.

Even on her toes, she wouldn't be able to reach his mouth unless he bent toward her.

His kisses made her forget about everything else in the world that wasn't them. For this time they spent together, nothing else mattered.

But the more time they spent together, the more she wanted.

Pulling away was torture but she forced herself to do it. At least, to try.

He let her go after a few seconds, his look curious when she opened her eyes.

"I know about RJ."

He went still for a second, not even breathing, before he sucked in a deep breath and took a step away.

"You want something to drink? I do."

"Brody—"

"Just...give me a sec, okay?"

She went silent as she followed him to the small kitchen, where he pulled a beer out of the fridge. He held out a second bottle, but she shook her head. She'd had enough to drink tonight.

Leaning against the counter, he took a swig and she broke her silence.

"I'm not asking you for information. That's not why I said anything. I just...want you to know you can talk to me."

She *wanted* him to talk to her, wanted him to trust her.

"How'd you find out?"

Trust went both ways, didn't it? "From a source in California. I can't tell you who. But I trust his information."

After another swig, he sighed. "I found out from my dad tonight at dinner. Now I'm wondering if you knew before me."

Shaking his head, he let his gaze fall away from hers, let it wander toward the windows looking out over the city.

"Would it matter?"

She took a few steps forward so she could stand beside him. She hadn't known him long but she knew he was upset. Not with her. He was upset with his dad. Or maybe just upset at the whole situation.

She wanted him to talk to her. Wanted him to *want* to tell her everything.

His gaze caught and held hers again. "Not to us. I'm not mad at you." He held out his hand and she took it, interlacing their fingers and letting him tug her closer. "This whole situation is just...fucked up."

"I can't imagine how tough it must be to work for your dad in this situation."

"I always knew it was a possibility, especially when the Colonials signed me. And I guess subconsciously I realized that would mean RJ would be here eventually. I guess...I don't know. I thought maybe it'd be a few years later?"

"Do you get along with your brother?"

"Yeah, actually, we do. It's just all the press bullshit—" He realized what he'd said a second too late to stop himself and grimaced at her. "Uh... Shit."

Laughing, she moved a little closer until their arms rubbed against each other, making her want to rub other parts of her body against him.

"You're cute when you're flustered."

Adorable, actually, but she didn't think he'd appreciate her saying so. How could a guy this tough and hard be so damn cute?

And when he laughed, low and deep in his chest... She could barely breathe.

"I'm not flustered. My mom just taught me better than to insult a lady. Even if she is a member of the press."

Her turn to laugh. And watch his gaze fall to her lips. He let his gaze linger for several long seconds until her nipples hardened and her thighs clenched.

She had to take a breath before she could speak again. "Have they given you a hard time?"

His gaze met hers again. "Not really, no. I just know that when RJ's here, I'm gonna get constant questions about how I feel playing with my brother and it's just gonna be a pain in my ass for a while."

Nodding, she gave him a commiserating grin. "I get it. People either see me as an unworthy successor to or a pale imitation of my dad when they first meet me. Either they get over it or they don't."

"Do they get over it?"

"Most of them. After a while. But yeah, it sucks. It's like having a spotlight shining on you that you don't want and can't escape."

"Exactly."

"I'd think you'd be used to the spotlight by now. You play for a major league team. People have been sticking a mic or a camera in your face for years."

He shook his head. "I don't think I'll ever get used to it. My dad and RJ, they know how to handle that shit. How to answer questions you don't want to answer without looking like an asshole. I don't have enough of a filter to do that. It made me question whether I wanted to play in the NHL or stay in the minor leagues."

Her fascination with him grew with every little nugget of information about himself that he passed on to her.

"Really? I mean...I guess I just figured it was every athlete's dream to play in the majors. The fame. The fortune."

"I'm not gonna say the money's not nice." He looked around at his apartment. "But, sometimes, I'm not sure the trade-offs are worth it."

He looked like he wanted to say something else but thought better of it.

She wanted him to talk to her. Didn't want him to hold anything back.

"Why?"

He paused, took a sip of his beer and stared into her eyes. "Because half the time you can't trust what people are telling you."

Was he implying that she was one of those people? That he didn't trust her?

Her thoughts must have shown on her face because he shook his head and raised his free hand to brush his fingers across her lips. Every part of her body from her scalp to her toes tingled with awareness.

"I trust you. Maybe I'm being stupid but..."

He didn't finish his sentence and she wasn't sure she wanted him to.

He shook his head. "Anyway, I wouldn't be completely upset if they moved me back down."

"To get away from all this stuff with your brother?"

"Maybe. Hell, I don't know. I just know I liked playing in Reading. I like the guys. I like the game down there. It's not that it's less stressful. I can handle the stress. It's just that the game's more..."

"Pure."

The minute the word left her lips, he smiled and her stomach hollowed out at the beauty of it. "Yeah, that's a good word for it. There's not so much bullshit."

Shifting from one foot to the other, she moved a little closer and suddenly, he pushed away from the counter.

"Shit, sorry. Let's go sit down. You sure you don't want something to drink?"

When she asked for some water, he grabbed a glass out of a

nearby cabinet and filled it from the pitcher in the fridge. Handing it to her, he grinned then led her out to the living area and the couch that played a big role in her recent dreams.

"So, you were out with friends before you came over?"

"Yeah, I met one of my best friends from work at some new place in Fishtown. It was nice. Good food. Better drinks."

"Felt the need for liquid courage before you faced the beast in his lair, huh?"

Falling into the way-too-comfy couch, she watched him sit next to her, careful not to crowd her.

Like she'd be able to forget he was there. Like he thought she'd be threatened by him. Or maybe he just didn't want to scare her away.

He didn't scare her away. Pretty much the opposite.

"You're not a beast. Although," she looked around at the wall of built-in bookcases behind the couch, "you've got the library for the part."

When he looked at her with a question in his eyes, she shook her head. "You never saw *Beauty and the Beast*?"

"The cartoon?"

"Yeah. It was one of my favorites as a kid."

"Not that I remember."

"Well, one of the ways the Beast wins over Beauty is by letting her have access to his huge library. I always wondered if he read all those books or just had them around for show. You've read all these books, haven't you?"

The look he gave her was tinged with humor. "Well, yeah. Why else would I have them sitting around?"

Setting her glass on the table so her hands were free, she moved a little closer to him and watched his gaze narrow.

"Guys who read are infinitely sexier than guys who don't."

"I read because I like it. I don't read on my phone, though. I like to hold a book in my hands."

The alcohol she'd consumed earlier loosened her tongue just enough.

"I like when you hold me in your hands."

It was probably a good thing he wasn't taking a drink at the moment because he might've spit it out, if the look on his face was any indication.

"You say things like that and I have to control the urge to spread you out on the couch and strip away all your clothes."

"And I'm probably going to let you." She held up a hand when he made a move toward her. "But first, I want to get to know you better."

"So you're telling me you want more than just sex?"

She bit her bottom lip, contemplating her next words carefully.

"And if I say yes? Is that what you want?"

He stared at her for several long seconds before he set his beer on the table next to her water and moved close enough that only inches separated their faces.

"I want whatever you're willing to give. But you've got to be willing."

She was willing. That was the problem.

"I don't think you understand how much of a complication you are to my life."

Her quiet words made him freeze.

Reaching up, she let her fingers trail along his jaw. He'd obviously stopped shaving in the past week and whiskers covered his cheeks and chin.

"I like this." She stroked his chin, stopping whatever words he was forming. "It suits you."

"Tara—"

"I talked to my editor. I told him about us. I can't cover anything to do with the Colonials. That makes this a problem for him. I don't like causing my editor problems."

"But you're still here."

"I am. I guess...I'm willing to give this a chance."

His gaze narrowed, that intense focus back in a major way.

"Good. Because I haven't had enough of you. And I haven't said that to anyone in my life."

He moved to put his hands on her waist and tugged her closer. Up onto her knees until her head was slightly higher than his and their breath mingled.

"And when you have had enough of me? What then?"

BRODY DIDN'T SAY the words on the tip of his tongue.

He knew he wasn't ready to say them, knew it wasn't the right time. Hell, he wasn't even sure he truly meant them.

But at this moment, he felt them.

I don't think I'll ever have enough of you.

He'd been in enough relationships to know this one felt different.

No, they hadn't spent much time together. Yes, this could still all fall apart, especially because they still had major issues that could trip them up, her job being a major one.

They also seemed to have a lot more in common than not.

And when she looked at him like she was now... He wanted to lock her down and tie her to him in any way he could.

Christ, they'd spent two nights together. Two.

But this was so different from anything else he'd experienced.

Kiss her, idiot. Stop obsessing.

Wrapping one hand around her neck, he pulled her down to kiss him.

When their lips met, and he felt her sigh, like she'd been waiting for him to kiss her forever, he let himself off the leash.

First, he let himself kiss her. For long, hot minutes, he

caressed her lips with his, building the heat between them with every second that passed. The hand around her neck tightened but he didn't pull her closer, just held her still. His other hand... Well, that one he gave permission to stray.

He set it on her shoulder, feeling the heat of her body seep through her clothing and into his palm. Into his bloodstream where she was already a virus.

Seconds later, he couldn't wait any longer. His hand slid down to cup her one breast, the soft mound making his stomach contract. Her back arched as she pushed herself into his hand, urging him to take the stiff peak he could feel beneath her thin shirt and bra and roll it between his thumb and forefinger.

He loved the sound she made when he did it, loved the way she kissed him harder, her tongue whipping against his.

Her hands rose to grip his shoulders before moving up to cup his head, her nails dragging along his scalp and raising goosebumps all over his body.

They'd both known they were going to end up in bed tonight but he didn't think either of them knew how very much they wanted that to happen.

The urgency that rose up between them made them almost frantic. Her hands fell back to his shoulders before she wrapped her arms around his back and tugged up his shirt.

She wanted to take it off. He had no problem with that. But she had to know he'd want the same from her.

When he released her breast, she made a little sound of longing deep in her chest. That sound made his cock throb behind the zipper of his jeans.

His fingers found the hem of her shirt and began to tug it up as well. By unspoken mutual agreement, they pulled away to strip off their shirts. Their gazes met and held for several seconds after their shirts hit the ground and the grin on her lips was a sight he didn't think he'd ever forget. Or ever be able to deny. That grin promised so much. And he was going to collect.

"Better take off the bra, too. Don't want to rip it."

Her grin widened as she reached behind to undo it. "Then I guess you better just strip down because I feel the same. Those jeans might not make it."

"Don't hurt my jeans. I like the way they fit."

Her gaze dropped to his lap for a second. "I do too."

Holy fuck. It was a damn good thing he'd shoved a condom in the back pocket of his jeans earlier because he had a feeling they weren't going to make it to the bedroom.

Hell, the fact that he had a condom in the pocket of his jeans pretty much made it clear he'd wanted to be prepared for anything.

The next few seconds became a race to see who could undress the fastest.

He won, but only because he wasn't wearing shoes. So by the time she got to her jeans, his hands were there to help.

Pushing her onto her back on the cushions, he tugged them down her thighs as she laughed. The sound made his blood thicken and his balls drew up hard.

Could he come from just the sound of her laugh? Fuck, he didn't want to find out.

Grabbing the condom from his jeans, he held it up to her, not bothering to wait for her to take it before he began to kiss his way down her body.

Starting at her jaw, he pressed open-mouth kisses along her soft skin, occasionally stopping to use his teeth. Sucking her nipples into his mouth in turn, he nibbled on her, feeling her squirm beneath him, her bare legs lifting to rub her inner thighs against his outer thighs. Giving him access to her sex.

One hand on her right hip, he put his other hand between her legs, two fingers sliding between her slick pussy lips. She groaned against his mouth as he flicked her clit then let one finger press inside her to stroke her high inside.

The sound she made now was one he'd hear in his dreams for months.

He hadn't thought he could be any more turned on than he was now. He'd been wrong.

His mouth sealed over hers as he continued to stroke her before pumping his finger inside her, then adding another and making her squirm even more.

He thought about getting her off first but he couldn't wait.

Pulling away to her disappointed moan, he grabbed the condom from her hand, ripped it open, and rolled it down his cock.

She reached to help but he shook his head.

"Nuh-uh. Reach up, hon. Grab the arm."

She obeyed without pause, her sleek body lengthening, inviting him to run his hands down the entire length of her torso to her hips. Arching beneath his hands, she gave him permission.

And he took it. Sliding one hand beneath her ass, he tilted her pelvis up. With the other, he aimed his cock then thrust forward, sinking deep and watching her face the whole time.

Her eyelids fluttered but didn't close completely. That connection seared him to his gut, making every muscle in his body tighten. Coming down over her, he held still inside her, fighting the urge to take her hard and fast.

Settling his mouth on hers, he kissed her, a deep, hot, wet lip-lock that drew a moan from her and shot a bolt of hot adrenaline straight through him.

Not moving, he absorbed the feel of her sex gripped tight around his shaft, the heat of her mouth and slight sting of her nails digging into his skin. He let the anticipation build, let the desire rise until he could barely contain it.

But when she began to swivel her hips, trying to create friction, to make him move, he had to give in. He couldn't deny her. Refused to deny her any longer.

Pulling out, he felt her legs tighten around his hips, trying to hold him inside. When he pushed back in, he felt her sigh in relief and welcome.

And then he unleashed his desire and fucked them both into oblivion.

EIGHT

"So you're dating Brody Mitchell, huh? Never got the chance to interview the kid myself but he seems a little...rough around the edges. His dad was one hell of an athlete. It'll be interesting to see how he handles the Colonials, especially with both of his sons playing for the team. Bold move, if you ask me. That kind of situation can be tough on your kids."

Tara's mouth dropped open a second before she managed to snap her jaws closed.

She shouldn't be a surprised that he knew. Still...

When her dad had texted her Tuesday morning to see if she was free for lunch the next day, she figured he just wanted to catch up. More than her other sisters, who met more often with their mom, Tara was a daddy's girl. Always had been.

But she'd been so busy, she hadn't really had time lately to talk to him. She'd either been covering a ball game...or spending time with Brody.

In the past week, they'd only managed to spend a couple nights together. But they'd talked or texted every day. And every day, she fell a little harder for him.

Which was something she didn't really want to examine too

closely, especially not with her dad at their favorite diner, where the owners knew Tara by name and always stuck a freshly made chocolate chip cookie in her bag whenever she got takeout.

"Who told you? Did Fleisch—"

"No, no. Of course not. Fleischer and I have known each other a lot of years but he'd never break a confidence like that. Not even to me. Rae squealed on you."

"Hmph. Figures."

She should've known her oldest sister wouldn't be able to keep a secret. Rae had called her two days ago to catch up. And when Rae had started asking her if she was seeing anyone, she'd broken down and told her about Brody just to shut down her questions.

Of course Rae would tell their mom and their mom would tell their dad.

"Now, don't be too hard on her," he continued. "I think it slipped out without her meaning to. The baby's been keeping her up nights and she's sleep-deprived. So, how'd you meet him?"

Well, damn. That was one hell of a loaded question.

"Can I ask you a question before we get to the inquisition?"

He gave her the dad look, the one she'd learned early on meant she should know better.

"If you were my editor and not my father, would you have fired me for dating Brody?"

His eyes widened. "Are you worried about being fired?"

"It crossed my mind, yes. I just need to know if Fleischer's giving me special treatment because I'm your daughter. But... you were friends with so many of the people you covered. Didn't you ever get pushback from people who said you were going easy on them?"

He shrugged, like she should've known the answer. "Yes, of course. But it's tough to be in this business and not make friends. You can't just divorce the different parts of your life. But I never had a, um, relationship like the kind you have with Brody."

Her cheeks burned with a blush. There was no way she was discussing her sex life with her dad. No way in hell. But she'd needed to talk to him.

"I guess I just need to know I'm not getting special treatment."

"I can't speak for Fleischer, but I can tell you I wouldn't have fired you for this. You told him immediately, right? That you were dating?"

When she nodded, he continued.

"If Fleischer had to fire every reporter who had a personal conflict, he wouldn't have any left. Life's messy, kid. You're a damn good writer and you continue to get better every day. He'd be crazy to fire you. Now, tell me. Is this relationship serious?"

She shrugged, her gaze skittering away for a split second. "We've only been seeing each other for a couple of weeks. And with baseball winding down, we haven't had that much time to spend together."

Another dad look. "You didn't answer the question."

No, she hadn't. Because she wasn't sure what she should say.

"Tare?"

"I don't know, Dad. It's...complicated."

"Aren't all relationships?"

She groaned and let her head fall back. "Why do you always have to be so flipping logical?"

He shrugged. "You'd think I'd been taken over by aliens if I wasn't."

"I can't believe I'm talking to you about this."

His eyebrows rose. "Would you rather talk to your mom? I'm sure she'd love to hear all about your love life."

Groaning again, she shook her head. "Not fair, Dad."

He laughed. "You know she'd be more than happy to talk to you about it."

A familiar pang of guilt hit her dead center in her chest. Tara adored her mom. She did. She just wasn't like her sisters, who had run to their mom with every new boyfriend and broken heart.

"I know. It's just..."

"You don't owe us every second of your life, honey. You're allowed to have a private life."

She grimaced. "That's part of the problem. Brody wants more. He doesn't want to be as private about our relationship as I do. But..."

"But what?" her dad prompted.

"What if it doesn't work out?"

"Then it wasn't meant to be. But what if it does? Or is that what you're afraid of?"

She wanted to say no, but she couldn't, not honestly.

"Sweetheart, maybe you're getting a little ahead of yourself. You're not going to run off and elope." Frowning, he looked at her a little closer. "Right? I mean, it's just been a couple of dates."

God, no, she wasn't going to elope. But it was so much more than just a couple of dates. Not that she could say that to her dad. Not without embarrassing the hell out of both of them.

She nodded, smiling. "You're right. It's just been a couple of dates."

And the growing sense that Brody was going to mean more to her than any other guy she'd dated.

"So, how's the new project going?"

Yes, it was a blatant attempt to turn the conversation away from her love life, but it was her only play. Thankfully, her dad let her get away with it.

But she knew Brody wouldn't take it as easy on her.

Are you free Saturday? Friends are having a housewarming. We're invited.

TARA STARED AT HER PHONE, knowing Brody had probably already checked the Phillies schedule and knew they were playing in Toronto.

She was working a rare Friday day shift to catch up on a few outstanding features and to do a phone interview for a Sunday piece on a local little league player with one arm who was a pitching ace.

Yes, she had the night free.

"Why are you staring at your phone like it's grown horns and a tail and is about to bite you?" Ethan leaned back in his chair, frowning at her from across the aisle. "Did someone die?"

Rolling her eyes, she sighed and placed her phone face down on the desk so Brody's question wasn't mocking her. Taunting her. Teasing her.

"No one died. Just... It's nothing."

Ethan's eyebrows rose. "Doesn't seem like nothing."

"Well, it is. I'm heading out for coffee. You want something?"

"Yeah, but I guess I'm gonna have to get coffee to find out the answer to my question."

Because that's exactly what she wanted, she got up and headed for the break room. Hopefully it'd be empty, but it was a newsroom. Someone was always drinking coffee.

Her luck held for a change. No one else was there and Ethan wasted no time.

"So, who was on the other end of that message?"

Leaning against the doorjamb as the lookout because he knew she didn't want anyone to overhear, Ethan crossed his arms over his chest and stared at her.

"Brody." She checked to make sure no one was in hearing range. "Because he wants me to go to a party with him tonight."

It took a second before a grin spread across Ethan's face. "That sounds serious."

"It's not. Not really. I just... We've only been dating a little while."

"Does Fleischer know?"

"Yes."

"Then what's the problem?"

"Maybe I just don't want everyone to know my business."

"Have you told *anyone*?"

"Lindsay knows." Ethan's mouth opened but she held up a hand to stop him before he could protest. "You weren't around the day I told her and then...I just..."

She shrugged, unable to find an excuse that would satisfy Ethan.

"Uh-huh." Ethan's expression held no hurt, which was what she thought he'd be. "You don't want people thinking you're sleeping with professional athletes. I get it. But hell, it's not like you're sleeping with the Phillies pitcher, for chrissake. You don't cover hockey. What's the big deal?"

"We've only been dating a couple of weeks and who knows if it's going to go anywhere."

"And by dating, you mean sleeping with."

"Yeah. I should've known it wouldn't be so easy as just a one-night stand. I swear I have the worst luck."

"Hey, if you don't like the guy—"

"That's not what I meant." She sighed heavily. "I like him. Maybe a lot."

"So what's the problem? Is he a dick? I mean I know some of them can be—"

"No, not at all. He's actually really great. We haven't known each other that long but—"

"But what?"

She hesitated. "But nothing. I can't think of a single 'but' to throw in there."

"Then don't. So what did he want?"

"His friends are having a housewarming. He wants me to go with him."

"Ooh, meeting the friends. Big step."

"And I'm sure they're all gonna be hockey players. Or at least most of them will be. And it'll get around that we're dating."

"And reality'll set in." Ethan shook his head. "You two picked a hell of a time to start a relationship."

"Yeah, our timing sucks. But...I think..."

"I think you say yes," Ethan's voice held a note of command, "and let the rest work itself out."

"There are so many ways this can go wrong."

"But the glass is also half full. Just think about that.

Before she could respond, Christine from advertising sailed into the room and she and Ethan made their way back to their desks.

Picking up her phone, she typed out her response before she overthought it.

I'd love to go. Send me details.

It didn't take him long to respond.

Great. Party starts at 7. Pick you up 6:45.

Half of her brain told her to tell him she'd meet him there. The other half wanted her to tell him to come a little early so they could make out before they left.

If she was going all in on this, she was going all in.

I'll text you my address.

She thought that'd be the end of it and set her phone down after she did so. But it pinged a few seconds later.

How's your week?

Busy. How's conditioning?

Honestly? Been better.

Does your shoulder hurt?

No. That's the one thing that doesn't.

A quick grin curved her lips. She wondered if he'd meant that as a double entendre or if she was just reading it that way?
A second later, she had her answer.

And yeah, that's exactly what I mean.

An actual giggle escaped her lips, drawing a glance from the sportswriter on the other side of the partition.
"You okay, Downey?"
"I'm fine."

Then I guess you're cleared for play.

We can leave the party early.

I'd be okay with that.

A short pause.

I missed you this week.

A pit opened in her gut, the wicked longing she'd been suppressing roaring through her on a rush of adrenaline.

Missed you too.

Good.

Well...damn. Her heart flipped in her chest.

You doing anything tonight?

She wasn't. As a matter of fact, she'd planned to do nothing tonight. Maybe subconsciously hoping he would ask her to get together.

No. Do you want to get together?

Yes. Come over.

It embarrassed her how fast she texted him back to say okay. But she wasn't trying to hide how much she wanted to see him. She'd literally just told him she'd missed him.
Yeah, you only want to hide it from everyone else.
She shoved that thought out of her head.

Okay. See you tonight.

With a sigh, she got back to work, hoping she'd be able to concentrate. Knowing she'd spend most of the day thinking about how she and Brody were going to spend their night.

Hopefully, most of it would be naked.

NINE

"RJ." Brody blinked. "What the hell are you doing here?"

"Nice to see you too, kid."

His mouth hanging open, Brody stared at his brother in shock. RJ had been the last person he'd expected to see at his door right now. Actually, the only person he'd wanted to see was Tara.

He'd told the doorman he was expecting her and to let her up immediately. Of course, all his brother had to do was give his name at the desk and he had immediate access, as well. All of his family did.

RJ's brows rose. "You gonna let me in?"

"Shit." Brody shook his head. "Yeah. Come on in."

Opening the door wider, Brody waved his brother in then returned RJ's hug.

"I wasn't expecting you until next week. Do Mom and Dad know you're here early?"

RJ shook his head. "No. I was actually hoping you and I could spend some time together tonight before I head over to the house tomorrow."

Well shit.

He was going to have to tell RJ the truth because Tara would be here in minutes.

If RJ was here, she'd insist on leaving.

"By the look on your face, I'm gonna say you have plans."

RJ sounded amused and maybe a little shocked.

Brody's brows lowered. "You make it sound like I never do anything."

"No, you know I don't mean that. I'm glad you're getting out and meeting people."

It was on the tip of Brody's tongue to tell RJ off. But he knew his brother would never be snarky. RJ was the proverbial boy scout. Loved by everyone. Always had the right words to say, always did the right thing. The guy was a paragon of fucking virtue.

Ugh. Brody shut down that train of thought. Sure, RJ was almost perfect but Brody loved him. RJ had always been there for him, no matter what.

"Actually, I'm not leaving my apartment."

When RJ looked at him strangely, Brody just stared back.

And his brother finally got it.

"You got a girl coming over? Really? Who is it? Mom didn't say anything—"

"You don't know her and they don't know we're dating so I'm invoking the Pact."

That last word evoked some of their oldest shared memories, when they were two brothers against the world. Or just against their parents and sister. RJ's lips curved in a smile.

"Damn. Seriously? The Brother Pact? She must be special."

"I think she is."

"Hey, that's great. I'm glad you're finally getting over that whole mess with Angelica. That girl was a bitch on wheels. I wish..."

Curious, Brody watched his brother for any hint to what he was thinking. "What?"

"I wish I could've done more for you there."

"Wasn't your mess."

"Yeah, but she fucked with you and I should've been there."

"I never needed you to fight my battles, RJ. But I always knew you had my back."

Something crossed his brother's expression, something Brody couldn't read. He got the sense that something was going on here but couldn't put his finger on exactly what it was.

But he also knew his brother.

"Hey, is something going on?" Brody asked. "Is there a reason you're here earlier than you're supposed to be?"

"Nah, just some plans fell through at the last minute in LA, so I figured I'd come out and get settled early. I'll head over to Mom and Dad's so I don't cramp your style."

RJ started for the door, his smile crooked.

"Wait—"

Another knock on the door. This time Brody knew it was Tara.

Shaking his head, RJ sighed hard.

"Jesus, my timing sucks lately."

Brody barely heard the words RJ muttered under his breath but heard the tone. Something was definitely going on with RJ. And it wasn't good.

He was torn between opening the door and getting his older brother to talk.

"Look, just give me a minute to tell Tara—"

"No. No way. You have plans. With an actual girl." RJ held up his hand and gave him a smile that was totally the RJ Brody knew. Confident. Teasing. Always upbeat. "I'm not messing with that. I'm here to stay for a while. We'll have a lot more time to talk. And I'm looking forward to it. But you have plans so have a good night, brat. I'll talk to you tomorrow."

Before Brody could respond, RJ opened the door.

"Oh. Oh, I'm sorry," Tara said. "I didn't—"

"He didn't either." RJ stuck out his hand to shake Tara's and pull her through the door. "Hi, I'm RJ, Brody's brother. You must be Tara. Nice to meet you."

Brody had a split second to wonder how Tara would react to his charismatic older brother. He saw her smile, saw her confusion then saw recognition set in.

"Nice to meet you, too. I didn't know you'd be here. Brody didn't say—"

"Brody didn't know. I just stopped to say hi. I'm leaving now. It was nice to meet you, Tara. Hope to see you again. Have a good night, you two."

Then RJ was out the door, leaving Brody and Tara staring after him like idiots with their mouths hanging open.

"I didn't think he'd be here so soon."

It took Brody a few seconds for the meaning of her words to make sense but when they did, his gaze narrowed.

"What do you mean?"

Her face twisted in a frown that made his heart stutter.

"I got a tip from a sports agent I know in LA that RJ had signed the contracts. Since I can't have anything to do with the Colonials at work, I passed it on to the other general assignment reporter."

"Were you going to tell me you knew?"

"Of course. I was—

"Sorry." Grimacing, he held up one hand in surrender. "Damn it. Not a fair question. RJ surprised me. I had no idea he was going to show up here tonight. Hell, I didn't even know he was home."

"Are you happy to see him?"

"Yeah." He thought about it for a second and realized he wasn't just saying what she wanted to hear. Or what he should be feeling. "Yeah, I am. He's always been there for me. I mean, the guy's perfect. If I needed the shirt off his back and his last dollar, he'd give it to me. Sometimes, I really wanna hate him but I can't. Makes me feel like even more of a dick."

"You're not a dick. I get it. Both of my sisters are older and they've always been pretty and perfect and girly. And then there's me."

"And what's wrong with you?"

She shrugged, and her expression turned rueful. "I'm just... not them."

"Good. I like you this way. You're you."

Her smile brightened. "I've kind of always felt like the ugly duckling compared to them."

"Then you're the sexiest fucking ugly duckling I've ever met."

Throwing back her head, she laughed and walked up to him, pressing herself against him and tucking her head under his chin. Her arms wrapped around his waist and he put his around her shoulders, loving the feel of her body against his.

"You're such a smooth talker."

He laughed, the heat of her body seeping into his and raising his blood pressure.

"That's such a total lie."

"I wish it was."

Before he got the chance to ask her what she meant, she kissed him and he forgot about everything except the need between them.

"HEY, it's Tara, right? I didn't have a chance to introduce myself yet. I'm Vivi."

Tara took the woman's hand, returning her bright smile with one of her own. "Hi, Vivi. It's nice to meet you."

"I think you already met my boyfriend, Justin."

Tara had met a lot of people tonight but she remembered the tall, quiet guy Brody had introduced as his former roommate in Reading. Tara had liked him immediately. His smile had been a little shy and he hadn't said much, but he'd seemed genuinely interested in her.

"I did. He seems really sweet."

Vivi laughed, nodding, but her expression when she glanced at her boyfriend was almost reverent. "He is. But don't tell him I said that. How long have you been seeing Brody?"

"Not long." And probably not for much longer, when he found out what she knew and hadn't told him... "We only met a few weeks ago."

"And you're a reporter, right? For one of the local papers?"

"Yes. The *Record*. I cover baseball and basketball."

"Sounds like fun."

This was usually the time when Tara gushed about how much she loved her job. Except today, she just wasn't feeling it. But she smiled and nodded. "Usually, yes."

Vivi's gaze narrowed and Tara realized this woman was a hell of a lot sharper than she'd taken her for at first glance.

The purple-tinged hair, tattoos, and unrestrained laugh had led Tara to make a snap judgment. Rookie mistake. This woman didn't miss a thing.

"But not today apparently."

"Today's one of those days where I question my calling." As soon as the words were out of her mouth, Tara shook her head. "Sorry. Forget that. So, everyone here seems to get on pretty well together. They all played together in Reading, right?"

Vivi didn't answer right away and Tara had the sense that

the other woman wasn't going to let her off the hook for that earlier comment. But they didn't really know each other so why would this woman even care what she had to say?

Finally, Vivi nodded and turned so she had the same view as Tara. "Yeah. It's a really great group. A few of the guys have been with the team for a couple of years. They've built a pretty strong bond. They weren't too sure of Brody at first but after a couple weeks, he fit right in. He never dated, though, so we've all been dying to meet you."

Tara's brows rose, which set off Vivi's laughter again.

"I'm not really that interesting."

"I think you're selling yourself short. Brody—"

"Viv. Don't cross-examine the poor woman. I'm sorry, we can't take her anywhere. Hi, I'm Aly and I'm almost embarrassed to admit this is my sister."

"And by embarrassed, she means terrified of what will come out of my mouth."

Aly's expression held a look Tara had seen more than once on her older sisters' faces. Loving exasperation

The banter between the women gave Tara a little breathing room.

When she and Brody had walked in, they'd been surrounded by several huge men and their women, who were unabashedly happy to see each other.

Everyone had been friendly, but they all knew each other so there were a lot of conversations going on at the same time. Tara had stuck close to Brody's side, trying to put names with faces and match girlfriends and boyfriends.

But a few minutes ago, when a redhead named Derek whose favorite word began with "F" started talking to Brody about the upcoming season, she excused herself to grab something to drink. Brody had been ready to come with her but she'd smiled and told him she'd be right back.

Truth be told, she'd needed a few seconds to breathe. She hadn't really known what to expect tonight but, even though she was a reporter, this kind of situation, where she knew no one, was stressful enough, especially for the introvert she truly was.

But add to it the information she'd learned about Brody's brother... She felt the beginnings of a headache building in her temples.

"I'm sorry, Tara. We're kind of chatty when we get together."

A newcomer to their little group, a woman named Faith, drew her attention back to the conversation. She'd joined Aly and Vivi a few minutes ago and the conversation had turned to Aly's new job at a major Philadelphia hospital.

"I'm enjoying it. I mean, it's a huge leap from Reading to Philadelphia but it's totally worth it to not have to drive from Reading every other day for a game or battle the damn Schuylkill Expressway on a Friday to spend the weekend with Riley."

"Did you want to leave your job?"

Tara could have kicked herself for letting herself blurt that out. And when all of the women in their little group turned to look at her, she wished like hell she could've kept her damn mouth shut.

She figured she was about to get the brush off for overstepping. She'd only just met these women. What the hell had she been think—

Then Aly's nose wrinkled and she shrugged. But her smile when she shook her head was honest and open.

"Honestly? Maybe not. But this new job is a step up and maybe I never would've taken that step if I hadn't wanted to be closer to Riley. What do you do for a living, Tara?"

"I'm a sportswriter for the *Record.*"

Aly's eyebrows rose. "Really? Do you cover the Colonials?"

"No. If I did, I'd be out of a job. Or I wouldn't be dating Brody."

Aly's brows rose even higher. "Damn. And here I am, complaining about getting a better job."

"But it's tough being in a relationship with a professional athlete, isn't it?" Tara's curiosity overcame her introvert tendencies. "I mean, it's gotta be tough to maintain your career when you never know if he's going to be traded or sign with another team. You have to pick up your entire life and start over, sometimes across the country or even overseas."

It took Aly a few seconds to respond, but when she did, Tara didn't get the impression she was offended or uncomfortable with Tara's question.

"True. To some people, it might look like I'm making all the sacrifices. But Riley won't play forever. He has a finite number of years to be at the top of his game. And I either had to come to terms with the fact that my life could be unsettled for the next ten or fifteen years or I let him go. I'd have my job but I wouldn't have Riley. I wasn't prepared to give him up. And he understands the sacrifices I'm making for him."

"It sounds like you guys have everything figured out."

Vivi snorted out a laugh that made Aly glare at her sister before it dissolved into a sheepish grin.

"Of course, we have issues. All couples do. You just have to learn to roll with them."

"And trust me," Vivi said, "it took them a while to figure out how to roll."

"Not that I tell her this often but Viv's right. It all comes back to communication."

Vivi and Faith nodded in perfect unison, as if Aly had just laid down the gospel.

Just then another woman entered their circle and the conversation made another turn.

Tara smiled and nodded when it seemed appropriate but her gaze wandered across the room to Brody.

He had that half grin on his face that she'd only seen him give his sister. Apparently, these people were more than just friends to him. He considered them family.

And what happened when he found out she knew why RJ had been more than happy to cross the country to come play for their dad? Would he understand that there had to be a delineation between her job and their relationship?

Or would he realize what she had already?

That sometimes you just couldn't save a relationship that had too many obstacles.

"MITCHELL. I can't believe I'm saying this but it's good to fucking see your ugly face, man."

"Hey, D. What trouble you get into lately?"

"Not as much as he could have." Sophie Tsoukalos gave Brody an enthusiastic hug and smacked a kiss on his cheek before stepping back and letting Derek Flaherty wrap his arms around her. "It's *so* good to see you. We're gonna miss you in Reading this year."

Shane and Bliss's party was in full swing about an hour after Brody and Tara had walked through the door of the couple's new apartment in Fairmount Park.

He'd kept Tara close at first, knowing how overwhelming this group could be. Everybody knew everybody else, except for Tara, so he didn't want her to feel abandoned.

When she'd smiled and told him she was going for a drink, he watched until he saw Viv approach her then he waited until Tara smiled.

And he let out a sigh of relief. That smile looked genuine.

He'd have to thank Viv later. And when Aly and Faith joined them, he gave himself permission to let her out of his sight.

"Yeah, well, hopefully this asshole will be in Philly this season." Brody grinned at Derek. "Rumor has it we're gonna need a few players."

"Yeah, I heard that same rumor. Your dad really gonna break up the Strakas?"

"He hasn't said anything to me but all you gotta do is look at the numbers. The cap's gonna take a hit with RJ's contract. He's gonna need to unload some players. The Strakas are obvious choices, especially considering the talent in Reading and Lancaster. And no one knows if Freddie's gonna play."

D-man Freddie Brockmeyer had been brought in last year to give the Colonials some muscle, but the older player had made some noise about retiring at the end of last season. He hadn't signed a contract yet

"Hey, enough about hockey for a few minutes," Sophie broke in. "I wanna hear about your date. Is she really a *Record* reporter? How's that gonna work during the season?"

"She doesn't cover the team. No conflict."

Brody automatically sought out Tara as Sophie peppered him with questions. He didn't mind answering but when he couldn't find her, he excused himself and set off in search of her.

He checked in with Vivi, who told him Tara had headed toward the kitchen.

When he didn't find her there, he checked the bathroom and then the bedrooms and came up empty.

Finally, he found her alone on the deck. The temperature still hovered around ninety degrees so no one wanted to be out in the sweltering heat.

Except Tara, apparently.

"Hey. Is something wrong?"

"It's beautiful out here," she said, not turning to look at him. "Your friends all seem great."

"Then why are you out here?"

"I heard about RJ."

Now she turned to look at him and the worry he thought he'd seen in her eyes earlier had turned into something resembling anguish. And even though her words made no sense, a hard ball of anxiety settled into his stomach.

"Tara, what—"

"I need you to know I didn't go digging for information. I got a call from a friend at a paper in LA. He wanted to know if I had any information to share. I told him I had no idea what he was talking about and it was true. But he told me about RJ."

"What are you talking about?"

Sighing hard, she shook her head and looked away. "I wasn't sure if you knew. I guess you don't. Damn it."

"Don't know what? What are you talking about?"

Although maybe he didn't want to know, if the look on her face was anything to go by.

Several seconds later, she sucked in a deep breath, as if gathering up her courage. "Two women have accused RJ and two other players of trying to buy their silence after a wild party where these women say they were molested."

Brody's heart stopped for a full second before it kicked into a furious beat. "No *fucking* way—"

"They're not accusing RJ of molesting them," Tara continued, "only of trying to cover it up."

"No. There's no fucking way RJ would've done that." Brody had absolutely no doubt he was right. RJ wasn't that guy.

Tara's expression didn't change. "I'm not saying he did it. I'm only telling you what the story is. Brody...this could get messy."

"Wait. How long have you known about this?"

Now, she looked guilty and his heart dropped into his gut. "A couple days."

The white noise in his head got a little louder.

"You knew." His voice held a note of control even he didn't recognize. "And you didn't tell me?"

"I *couldn't* tell you. There's a difference and you know it. I was told that information in confidence—"

"And you didn't trust me to keep my mouth shut?"

"No, Brody, that's not what this is about."

He snorted. "Yeah, I think it is. You don't trust me. Your job comes first."

As soon as the words were out of his mouth, he knew they were the wrong ones.

Tara looked like she'd taken a low blow. "That's not fair. We agreed. We don't talk about the Colonials. That's the only way this relationship works."

"He's my brother."

"And it's his story to tell."

"Apparently not if the newspaper gets their hands on it first."

"I passed the information along to Sean. I'm not writing the story. What was I supposed to do with the information? Run it by you first? If RJ had told you what happened, would you have told me?"

"Of course not. He's my brother. He's entitled to some fucking privacy."

"Except this isn't a private matter. This directly affects his ability to do his job. He's a public figure. You know that. If this were anyone other than your brother, would you be this upset?"

TARA WAITED a beat for Brody to answer but he stubbornly kept his mouth shut.

Feeling her stomach clench into a ball, Tara shook her head. "I would have never broken your trust because that's not who I am. But apparently you don't know that."Heart pounding against her ribs, she took a deep breath and spoke the words that tasted bitter on her tongue.

"This isn't going to work."

His jaw tightened into granite. "Tara—"

"Don't." She held up one hand between them. "I'm leaving. If I stay..."

The silence grew between them like a living thing as she tried to get her feet to move. She didn't want to leave because she knew if she did, she'd probably never see him again. And that opened a huge, aching pit in her stomach that threatened to make her ill.

"What, Tara?" Brody broke the silence with his gruff response. "If you stay, you'll say something you'll regret? Or is there something else you haven't told me?

"Don't. Just don't. Don't say anything else because if you do, you're going to say something you can't take back."

"What have I said that I should take back? Tell me what I said that isn't true."

She had to unclench her jaw to speak. "You're right. You're absolutely right. There's nothing else to say."

Except she was pretty sure he had something else to say. She had no idea what it would be. But she was pretty sure she didn't want to know.

You should've known this would never work out.

It never did. She'd been so foolish to think they could make this relationship work when everything seemed to be stacked against them.

He didn't say another word as she walked away, grateful she didn't have to walk through the house again to get to the street where an Uber would take her away.

TEN

"Jesus, RJ, why didn't you tell me?"

His brother ran a hand through his normally perfect hair, his expression pained.

After Tara had left the party, Brody had texted Shane, told him he'd had to leave and that everything was okay.

Except nothing was okay, apparently.

"I was going to," RJ finally said. "Honestly, I was going to tell you but there never seemed to be a good time. And then the reporters started to call, and Dad and Gabby and I decided not to drag you into this mess."

"Did you tell Mom?"

"Of course."

"Then you should've told me."

"I know. I realize that now but I didn't want to put you in the situation of having to lie to your girlfriend."

That one hit him like an ice pick in the gut. "Not sure I can call her that anymore."

RJ looked stunned. "Because of this shit? Goddammit." He banged his hand against the door hard enough that Brody heard it crack. "This is what I was trying to avoid. And you got dragged into this shit anyway. *Sonuvabitch.*"

"I'm sorry. Tara didn't tell me—"

"Of course, she didn't tell you. It wasn't her job to tell you—Wait, is that why you're not seeing her anymore? Because she didn't tell you?"

When Brody didn't answer, RJ closed his eyes and shook his head, looking even more pissed than he had before.

"Christ, when I fuck shit up, I fuck it up good. Dude, this is not her fault. You know that, right? This is my fault. I made a stupid mistake for what I thought was the right reason and of course it blew up in my face. You need to apologize to Tara and beg her to take you back."

"Probably better this way. It was never going to work anyway."

"Do you want it work?"

Hell, yes, he'd wanted it to work. The past several weeks with her in his life had been amazing. Maybe the best of his life.

"Brody?"

"You know, somedays I kind of feel like I'm an afterthought or a consideration."

"What the hell are you talking about? No one—"

"You just told me you didn't want to drag me into this shit. That you didn't want fuck up my life. But you fuck up my life when you don't tell me what the hell's going on. You make me feel like I'm living on the periphery of this family."

"Shit, Brody, that wasn't anyone's intention."

"I know that. I'm just fucking sick of feeling like it."

RJ closed his eyes and shook his head. "All I can say is I'm sorry. And don't let my utter fucking stupid life choices cause you to lose someone special."

"She walked away so I'm guessing she doesn't think I'm special enough to stay."

His brother's eyes opened and locked onto his. "Do you really believe that or are you just being an asshole?"

"Aren't I normally?"

"Stop feeling so fucking sorry for yourself and work it out with her."

"I'm not sure there's anything left to work out."

"Are trying to tell me you're afraid of failing?" RJ's mocking expression made Brody's back straighten. "You have *never* failed. You've always picked yourself up, no matter what. When people would compare you to me, you always made them rethink their bullshit. You had what could've been a career-ending injury. You came back stronger. You won a fucking Calder Cup. And this year, we're gonna make a run for the Stanley Cup. Together."

"And that's what I should be working toward. I should keep my mind on the game, not on a girl."

"Why can't you do both? Other people do it all the time."

"I just don't know if we can work it out. I don't know how to start."

RJ smiled, a true smile, the first Brody could remember since RJ had gotten here.

"Put in the work, man. Start with the basics and work your way back up. And don't let my shit drag you down."

"ALL RIGHT, Downey. You need to snap out of this funk. I get that you're depressed over your breakup with he-who-shall-not-be-named but it's been two weeks. You need an intervention. Or to get laid and put the asshole out of your head."

"Don't have time for either. I have a game tonight and tomorrow I have to cover training camp for Sean."

Ethan's eyes widened. "Seriously? Fleischer assigned you to cover the Colonials? Willingly?"

"He didn't have anyone else and since I'm no longer dating anyone on the team..."

Ethan's brows rose so high, she thought they might actually disappear. "And you think that's a good idea?"

"It's my job and I'm the only one available."

"Sounds like you're torturing yourself, if you ask me. You know if you ask Fleischer—"

"I'm not asking Fleischer for anything. Like you said, it's been two weeks." She shrugged. "I have to get over it."

"Uh-huh." Ethan's tone held high-test sarcasm. "Next time, you might want to sound a little more convincing."

As Ethan rolled back to his cubicle, Tara returned her attention to the article she was writing. But she couldn't concentrate.

Ethan, damn him, was right. She needed to move on. Too bad she couldn't convince herself to do it.

Not when Brody had called three nights ago.

He was on the road with the team for a preseason game, which she only knew because... Well, shit. Because she'd memorized the Colonials' entire damn schedule. They hadn't spoken since the night they'd fought. She'd picked up her phone innumerable times to text him, to say... What? What would she say?

Nothing had changed.

She'd been covering a game so she hadn't been able to answer. He hadn't left a voice mail.

Which made her feel worse than she had before he'd called. If he'd wanted her to call him back, he would've left a message, right?

Ugh.

They'd both had time to cool down. She'd had time to cry. But she still hadn't figured out what they could do differently.

She still worked for the paper and he still played for the Colonials.

Maybe you just don't want to make it work.

She knew as soon as she thought the words that it wasn't true. She did want to make it work. She just didn't know how.

So she'd thrown herself into work with a determination that her boss had appreciated even while he watched her with a narrowed gaze.

She couldn't decide if Fleischer was waiting for her to break down or screw something up. So far, she'd hadn't done either.

But every day it got a little harder to pretend she was okay.

She *missed* him.

And now she had to cover the Colonials' practice today. She hadn't been lying when she'd said Fleischer had no one else to cover today. Yes, she could've begged Russo to switch their days off, but she wouldn't be able to avoid Brody for the rest of her life.

It'd get easier with time. It would.

She hoped.

"DUDE, who's the new chick reporter? She's a hell of a lot better to look at than any of the old men who usually cover us."

Brody didn't have to look at the press box to see who Tank was talking about. He'd seen Tara the second she'd walked in.

He'd almost skated over to talk to her but had stopped himself before he made a move.

He was still kicking himself for not leaving a message when he'd called her three nights ago. If she'd answered, he would've figured out something to say, but faced with that *beep* and then nothing... He hadn't known what to say.

He wanted to heal this rift between them, which meant he

needed to make the first step. Because she'd been right. And he'd let his hurt get in the way of seeing she was right.

He hadn't expected to see her here and he'd been able to keep his mind on practice, but now that Tank had mentioned her name, he couldn't stop from glancing up.

She was laughing up at the guy next to her. Since the guy was probably twice her age, Brody wrote off the twinge in his gut as a muscle cramp. Definitely not jealousy.

"She is new." Hubert Straka grabbed a water bottle from behind the boards. "With *Record.* Might be worth aggravation your sister will give me to get her in bed."

A couple of the guys gathered around for a water break rolled their eyes, but none of them paid Hugh much attention. The guy had an ego the size of the state but he backed it up with skill. His twin brother, Christian, had just been traded to Florida so everyone was cutting him a little slack. It wouldn't last long, though, because the guy rubbed a lot of people the wrong way.

Brody had to bite his tongue against the urge to tell Hugh to back the fuck off. He didn't want that asshole to talk about her, much less look at her. But if Brody opened his mouth, the guys would be all over him. A lot of the guys knew he and Tara had broken up. They didn't know why, they just knew Brody didn't want to talk about it. So they didn't.

"I'm pretty sure any woman who covers the team knows to stay the hell away from you." Mikki Lindback slashed Hugh across the back of his legs, not hard enough to hurt, just enough to make his presence known. "For fuck's sake, asshole, don't you know you shouldn't fuck anyone who can make your professional life a living hell?"

Hugh's shit-eating grin caused Brody's hand to curl into a fist. He quickly relaxed it before anyone could notice.

"That is what makes life interesting. Did I tell you about the woman Christian and I met in St. Croix? She was very—"

Brody turned and skated away. He had to tune the guy out; otherwise, he really would hit him just for being an asshole. And that wouldn't be a good way to start the new season. Not for him or his dad, who still had to deal with RJ's mess.

Christ, his sister would be all over his ass, and with RJ's shit still to hit the fan—

"Hey, Brody. You okay?"

Looking over his shoulder, he saw Lad closing on him. He and Lad had spent most of the day paired for drills so it was a pretty good guess that the rumor they were going to be on the second defensive line for the opening game was true.

"Yeah, just don't need to listen to Straka talk about sex with his brother."

Lad laughed at Brody's deliberate mischaracterization but didn't immediately skate away.

"He is asshole." Then he shrugged. "He gets off fucking with people's head. Ignore him."

That was an absolute truth. The problem was Brody's head wasn't screwed on as tight as it should be right now. Not with Tara in eyesight.

"Hey, you wanna grab dinner tonight?" Brody needed a distraction. "Don't know if any of the other guys are free but I could use a night out to blow off some steam. Maybe get to know a few of the new guys."

"Like in the biblical sense?"

Brody snorted at Ian Clark's stupid-ass comment. The guy was one of several Redtails up for training camp, although talk was the guy wouldn't be in the AHL long. Ian had proven himself to be a solid points scorer last season and Brody was pretty sure Ian would earn himself a spot on the fourth line soon after if not before the start of this season, even though Ian was one of the youngest guys in the system.

Outweighing Ian by at least fifty pounds and towering over him by five inches, Lad put his arm around Ian's shoulders, dwarfing the kid.

"You are small enough to crack like walnut, Clark Kent. I would watch your words carefully or I will make you eat them."

With the demented grin of the teenager he'd been only months ago, Ian rammed his shoulder into Lad's side, which barely made Lad twinge.

"I guess that's better than eating—*oof*. Dude!"

"Jesus, Ian, I leave you alone for two fucking seconds." Derek grabbed Ian by the arm and dragged him toward the locker room, where they were all headed. "Mind your manners or we're gonna have to put the muzzle back on."

Colin Williams and Riley Hatch laughed as they caught up to the guys before they got off the ice.

"Come on, kid, before you lose any of those baby teeth." Riley mock-shoved Ian in front of him and away from Derek. "You've got interviews. You don't wanna have to explain a bloody lip."

As the guys filed off the ice, Brody waited on the side with Lad.

"What time tonight?" Lad asked.

For a second, Brody couldn't help himself. His gaze went to the press box, where the local stringer for a national sports channel leaned just a little too close to Tara. He could tell, even from this distance, that she wasn't comfortable with how close the guy was. While he watched, he saw her do a quick sidestep and head for the exit.

"Why do you not just talk to her?"

Brody sighed in response to Lad's surprisingly quiet question. "Because I'm not sure she'd listen to anything I have to say."

"I've been telling him to call her, but he won't listen to me."

RJ skated to a stop beside him and Brody dragged his attention away from Tara to look at his brother. If you knew RJ at all, you'd know something was definitely wrong with him. Luckily for RJ, he didn't know a lot of these guys personally. So until the story broke, RJ could pretend to be just another one of the guys.

"Because it's shit advice."

"I do not believe advice is shit. You should talk to her."

"And say what?"

"That you are asshole," Lad said.

That actually got a grin out of RJ. "You could start there, at least."

RJ headed down the hall, leaving Brody with Lad.

"Talking's not gonna solve our problem."

"No, but it would be start."

Shaking his head, Brody had had enough. "So. Dinner. We doing this or not?"

"Yes. We will do dinner. I found Russian place off Roosevelt Avenue. Food is almost as good as my mother's."

"Yeah, sure. Text me the address and I'll meet you there. Ask whoever you want. I'll say something to Derek. The rest of the team'll know in five minutes. Six-thirty okay?"

Lad nodded slowly. "Are you sure you have nothing else to do tonight?"

Unfortunately no.

"Nah. Just have a lot on my mind."

"Then we should have much to talk about."

"There you are." Gabrielle appeared at the end of the hall to the locker rooms. "I need you both for interviews. I had hoped you'd be showered by now but I guess that was too much to hope for. Drop your gear, run through the shower then come over to the conference room."

Without waiting for them, she disappeared again, knowing they'd follow.

"Your sister. She is not dating, is she?"

Brody's brows rose as his brain tried to process what Lad was trying to say.

"Dude. Don't even."

Lad's elusive grin made an appearance. The guy had the whole stoic Russian thing down.

"I am only asking question. We can discuss tonight."

"I am *not* discussing my sister with you, man."

"Then we will find other things to talk about. We will discuss your problem with Tara. Now we should go or your sister will kick our asses."

Lad headed down the hall to the locker room before Brody could tell him to mind his own damn business.

But then he couldn't help himself.

He turned. And caught Tara's gaze before she could look away.

The longing in her eyes caught him off guard but she turned and practically ran away before he could respond.

"COACH, can you talk a little about your line pairings?"

Coach Angstadt took a few seconds before responding to the question from the local TV reporter.

Tara jotted notes, hanging in the back of the crowd of reporters, hoping like hell she wouldn't have to ask any questions,

So far, the press had questioned Coach about the overall play, but most of the reporters in the press box tonight had been particularly impressed with a few of the new faces in the lineups.

"Can you talk a little about your defensive pairings, especially Marchenko and Mitchell and Flaherty and Copley?" the ESPN correspondent next to her asked. "Are you going to keep them together for the start of the season and are you considering moving Flaherty up from the Redtails?"

Coach paused again before answering, his gaze steady. And when he spoke, she couldn't tell if he thought she had insider information. Which she did.

"I'm really happy with how those pairings worked out tonight. Marchenko and Mitchell have some timing issues to work on, but they'll be paired together Wednesday night. I don't have plans to split up Copley and Wysocki on the first line for the regular season, but I wanted to see how Flaherty held up against a more seasoned player. I'm pleased to say he held up well, as I'm sure you all agree."

With a nod, he moved on to the next question about special teams. As the post-game Q&A wound down and Coach finally left the stage, Gabrielle ushered those reporters who wanted to talk to particular players back to the green room for interviews.

Brody and Lad were available, along with Flaherty and Copley. She'd asked Gabrielle for a few minutes with Denis Copley and had gotten a cool response. Or maybe Tara was imagining things.

Copley had been around a while, had his answers down pat so it took less than a minute to ask her questions.

When she found herself face-to-face with Lad, she had to shove down the well of sadness that rushed up. She'd liked Lad when they'd met the other night but now... She wasn't sure how he'd respond to her. She hadn't really planned on talking to him but knew it would look funny if she'd only talked to one player for the article.

So she treated him like every other player, even as she wanted to ask him how Brody was doing.

"So what do you think you and Brody will be able to bring to the team?"

The hulking Russian defenseman took a few seconds to think then gave her a surprisingly detailed and intelligent response.

Tara's pen flew across the page of her notebook, but she had to make a conscious effort to keep her attention on him and not the man being interviewed by a walk-and-talk across the room.

If she kept her back turned to him, she could almost pretend Brody wasn't there. Except every now and then she'd catch a hint of his voice and it would make her brain stumble.

She didn't think Lad noticed. Then again, maybe she was fooling herself. Maybe they didn't know exactly what had happened, but they certainly knew she and Brody weren't seeing each other any longer.

After a couple more questions, she thanked him for his time.

He nodded and said, "It is nice to see you again, Tara. I hope it is not the last time."

Her gaze flashed to Brody, still talking to the female on-air reporter who looked like she'd just stepped out of a makeup trailer. Since the other woman didn't have a microphone stuck in Brody's face, Tara assumed they weren't taping.

The woman appeared to be doing all the talking while Brody looked like a trapped animal, getting ready to gnaw off a limb to get away.

Tara wondered if the other woman was oblivious to his reaction or just didn't care.

A split second later, Brody glanced her way and caught her staring. Their gazes held for several long seconds, while every second they'd spent together ran through her mind.

From across the room, she felt that spark flare between them. The one neither of them could do anything about.

She dragged her gaze back to Lad, whose sharp blue eyes missed nothing.

Shit.

"I will send Mitchell over to talk to you," he said. "I don't believe you have spoken to him yet."

"Oh no, that's okay. I don't—"

"Is no problem." Lad waved away her opposition with one hand, still grinning. "I am sure he will have much to say about our partnership. Besides, he looks as if he needs to be saved."

Her cheeks flamed as Lad turned and headed for Brody.

"Hello, Miss...?"

Saved.

She turned with a smile to see who'd rescued her and had to force herself not to take a step away.

Hubert Straka stood close enough that she could smell his deodorant. In other words, too close. She'd been warned by the Colonial beat reporter about him and his brother, recently traded to make room for RJ. He'd made a point of telling her to make sure she was never alone with either of the Straka boys.

"They take no prisoners," Sean Simmons had told her, shaking his head. *"Surprised they haven't been arrested or died yet."*

Usually, she nodded and privately rolled her eyes at that advice, the kind they usually only told women reporters. But this time, she got the feeling she should take it to heart. Because the look on Hugh Straka's face gave her the impression all the stories were true. Taking the hand he held out to her, she forced herself not to flinch away when they shook.

"Tara Downey. Nice to meet you, Mr. Straka."

"I understand you are new. I will take it easy on you this first time."

She caught an eye roll in mid-formation. Better not to give him any ammunition. Or encouragement.

"Straka. Channel Six wants you."

She stiffened. She couldn't help it.

Brody's voice came from behind her and every muscle in her body seized with anticipation as he stopped next to her. Her breath hitched, as it always did when she found herself near him.

For a second, she forgot they weren't together anymore. That she wouldn't get to leave here and meet him tonight at his apartment, like a normal couple.

She wanted that. And it wasn't going to happen.

A wave of sadness hit her and she wanted to turn and walk away and not deal with this situation. But she had a job to do. Wasn't that part of the reason they'd broken up?

"Hi."

"Hey."

A little silence fell, fraught with all the things they couldn't say.

Finally, she took a breath. "You and Marchenko played well together today."

She wasn't sure he was going to let her make small talk just to show they could. Then he sighed and ran a hand through his still-wet hair. He couldn't have done more than finger-combed it after getting out of the shower because it stood up in all directions. He looked like he hadn't shaved in days, his jaw covered in dark stubble that made her want to run her palms against it.

And his eyes... His eyes bored into hers with the knowledge of what they'd shared.

She swallowed hard and his gaze dropped to her throat.

"Helps to have a good partner. Makes everything go more smoothly."

There was that damn hitch in her breath again.

"I'm sure you're going to have a great season."

"Thanks." A pause. "Hey... Can we talk? Not here, obviously. Somewhere we can be alone."

She wanted to say yes. But nothing had changed.

She put on a professional smile that made his gaze narrow.

"I don't think that would be smart."

Crossing muscled arms over muscled chest, he nearly made her drool. She wanted to bop him over the head with her notebook.

"Okay, I guess I can say what I need to say here."

Her eyes widened and she shook her head.

"No, you can't." She dropped her voice to be sure no one could hear her. "I'm pretty sure you said everything you needed to say the other night."

"And probably a lot of shit I shouldn't have said."

Damn him, why did his voice do such amazing things to her body? It just wasn't fair, goddammit.

"I'm pretty sure you meant every single word." She held up a hand before he could say anything else. "No. I can't do this. I'm working."

"Then ask me about work."

Right. She was here to do a job. "Tell me about your new partnership with Marchenko. How do you think it's going to go?"

"I think our styles mesh well together. We both like to hit hard and go deep. We're not afraid to shoot the puck when we get the chance. We're going to give the team a solid second line that's going to produce points."

Now she felt like he was treating her like every other reporter there.

And it sucked.

"Sorry to interrupt, Ms. Downey, but did you get everything you needed? We're wrapping things up for the day."

Gabrielle appeared from behind her, a pleasantly detached smile on her face.

Of course. She'd become the enemy.

Shaking her head, she stuffed her notebook and phone back into her purse and flashed a forced smile.

"Didn't mean to hold everyone up. Time got away from me."

"You didn't." Brody's voice held that slight growl that made her skin tingle. "If you have any other questions, you know where to find me. Nice to see you again, Ms. Downey."

Then he nodded to his sister and headed back to the locker room.

She couldn't help herself. She watched him the whole way.

"I THINK you should tell your side of it before this whole situation blows up in your face. Get out in front of it."

"*You* think I should talk to media?" RJ looked stunned.

Brody took another swallow of beer as he and RJ sat on the couch in Brody's condo. They'd been spending a lot of time together now that RJ was in the same city. Probably because RJ was lying low and Brody just didn't want to deal with people. They'd been working out together, eating together, spending a hell of a lot of ice time together. It almost felt like they were kids again, except for the fact that Brody wasn't chasing after his older brother. Now they were on equal footing.

"No, I think you should talk to *one* member of the media. Someone you can trust. Ask Gabby to set you up with one of the local reporters."

RJ set his beer on the table in front of him and turned so he could face Brody directly. "Are you telling me to talk to Tara?"

Shaking his head, Brody nearly choked on his beer. "Hell

no. Don't drag her into this. But I think you need to tell your story before people start to distort it."

"I don't know. Maybe it'll just blow over."

"I don't think you can stick your head in the sand over this one." Brody drank the rest of his beer and set his bottle next to RJ's. "I think you need to just say, 'Hey, I fucked up. I'm sorry.'"

"I will if you will."

"What do you mean?"

"Oh, come on. You know exactly what I mean. You screwed up. Go tell her you're sorry."

"I don't think it's that easy."

"Nothing ever is. But you're right. I can't stick my head in the sand anymore. And if you want Tara, then neither can you."

"UH, TARA?"

Ethan's voice barely penetrated her concentration but she heard something in his tone that made her head pop up.

"What's wrong?" She frowned at him, noting his wide eyes. "You look—"

"What's RJ Mitchell doing here? With the whole Mitchell family? Walking your way?"

Her head swung toward the entrance.

Holy shit. Ethan was right.

Eyes wide, she watched Duncan, RJ, Gabrielle, and Brody make their way toward the sports department. Her gaze locked with Brody's, she watched him come closer. She barely noticed as his family peeled away several feet from her because he kept coming straight for her.

"Can we talk?"

Her heart racing, Tara stood, not sure what she should say.

She wanted to say yes but she had no idea what he wanted

to say. In her peripheral vision, she saw RJ, Duncan, and Gabrielle talking to Sean Simmons and her boss, who gave her a quick glance before ignoring her again.

"You want to talk? Now? About what?"

"Yes, now. I owe you an apology. I'm sorry. I was an asshole."

Her heart skipped a few more beats as he said what she'd been waiting to hear for days. What she'd feared he'd never say. But she had no idea why he was here now. What had changed?

What she did know was that she didn't want an audience for this conversation and she was pretty sure Ethan and Lindsay were staring at them unashamedly, as almost everyone else in the newsroom split their attention between RJ and Brody and her.

"Brody, let's go—"

"No, I kinda need to say this here. In front of...people."

Her eyes widened because she knew how much he hated being the center of attention. She also knew hope was a four-letter word.

"Our personal lives are no one's business but our own but you've got to know I respect the hell out of you. I think you're smart and dedicated and a few other things I'm not gonna say now."

Behind her, she heard Ethan cough over a laugh. Lindsay wasn't as coy. She outright snorted.

"Brody—"

"I miss you. I want to be with you. I'm sorry I was an asshole. Let me try to make it up to you. Give us a chance to work this out. I know how much your work means to you and I will never doubt your intentions again. I hate being apart from you and I think we make a great team."

Her eyes widened and her heart flipped over.

"I miss you, too."

His smile nearly made her melt into a puddle of goo and she was pretty sure she heard Lindsay snort again and Ethan sigh, though she couldn't drag her gaze away from Brody's.

Stepping forward, he got close enough that he could speak to her and no one else could hear.

"Then meet me at Haven for dinner at seven and I'll try to make up for the mess I made."

"It wasn't all your fault. I—"

"No, none of this is your fault. I'm the one who screwed up. I didn't trust you and I'm sorry. I can't say I won't ever screw up again because I'm not perfect. But I can promise that I'll try to be more evolved."

Her smile widened and the heat in his eyes felt like a sizzle on her skin.

"Don't evolve too much. I like you a little feral."

Now he leaned closer, his next words for her only.

"And I like you naked."

Every nerve ending in her body lit on fire.

"Tonight," he promised.

That was a promise she knew he'd keep.

ARE you really going to do this?

Hell yes, she was going to do this.

Tara pushed open the door to the private dining room at Haven and walked through, spotting Brody immediately.

He stood by the window looking out into the atrium but turned as soon as he realized she'd stepped into the room.

And when he smiled, she swore every cell in her body did a little happy dance. Her own smile felt too wide for her face but she didn't care if she looked ridiculous because they were here, together. Alone.

"Hi."

"Hey."

Crossing the space between them, he didn't stop until he stood right in front of her. Actually, he didn't stop until he was pressed tight against her. Then he wrapped his arms around her and dropped his mouth onto hers, kissing her until she could barely breathe.

He took his time, his lips firm against hers, tongue licking at hers, encouraging her to let him kiss her deeper, harder. Which she did.

Why wouldn't she when this was all she'd dreamed about since they'd broken up? When every part of her body yearned to be pressed against him?

Rising onto her toes, she pressed herself against him even more tightly, her mouth opening a little wider to give him even more access.

His arms tightened around for several long seconds, but then he started to pull away. She clung but it was obvious he wanted to either say something or breathe. Since breathing was fairly necessary, she let him go. Reluctantly.

Staring down at her, his gaze burned with the promise of what was to come. Her lips curved thinking about what the night held for them.

"If you keep smiling at me like that," he finally said. "we won't get to eat dinner."

"I'd be okay with that."

Brody's grin softened but the heat in his eyes didn't abate. At all.

"Me too. But I need you to know this relationship isn't just about sex. I don't want you to think that's all I'm after. I was serious earlier about making up for the mess I made. Because I totally made a mess of things."

"You're not the only. This situation isn't all your fault. We've got issues to work on but we can figure it out."

"I want to. I know we will." He paused for a second and she could tell he wanted to say something else. Then he sighed and released her. "Can we sit? Maybe having a table between us will help me say what I need to say."

She nodded, willing to work with him because he obviously had something he needed to say. When they were seated at the table, he took a deep breath.

"I know I said I was sorry earlier but I need to say it again. I'm sorry. Being with you makes my world brighter."

Tears burned at the corners of her eyes. She hadn't known what to expect from him tonight, but declarations like that had never really crossed her mind. And now that he'd spoken those words and they were ingrained in her brain, she wasn't sure he hadn't just melted her heart completely.

"How do you manage to do this to me?"

"What do you mean?"

His bemused expression made her smile widen.

"I mean," she rose from the chair she'd just sat on and eased herself onto Brody's lap, "that you say a few words and I'm ready to forgive you anything."

His expression didn't lighten, though he did settle his hands on her hips and hold her still. "I don't want you to have to forgive me. I'm going to try to be more enlightened and less feral."

He sounded sincere but his hands started to wander. One stroked up and down her back, sending shivers of desire through body. The other splayed across her upper thigh, his fingers dangerously close to a part of her anatomy that really wished they'd shut up and get naked.

But she certainly was enjoying what he had to say.

"I told you. I like you feral."

Now, he got that look in his eyes, the one that made her thighs clench and her core ache.

Against her hip, his erection hardened even more, and she scrambled to her feet. Before he had time to protest, she straddled his lap, wrapped her arms around his shoulders and pressed her mound against that hard ridge. Right where she wanted him to be. Without all these clothes between them.

His voice rumbled out of his chest. "You're about to find out just how much I'm not afraid to take you up on a dare."

"Oh, I'm not daring you." She leaned in close and put her lips right against his. "I'm flat out giving you permission. You want to make up with me? Take me. Make me come. I want you."

His groan echoed in the small room, sending her heart into an even rougher beat, his hands tightening on her hips almost painfully.

"Fair warning, I'm playing for keeps."

His words made her heart do a little happy dance.

"Good. Because I have no intention of letting you get away this time."

He pulled so he could look into her eyes and the expression on his face made her breath catch in her chest.

"Good. Because I love you, Tara. And I never—"

She sealed her lips over his and kiss the rest of his words away.

"I love you, too. And I won't—"

His mouth covered hers this time and he was good to his word. He didn't let her get away.

ALSO BY STEPHANIE JULIAN

REDTAILS HOCKEY
The Brick Wall

The Grinder

The Enforcer

The Instigator

The Playboy

The D-Man

The Machine

INDECENT
An Indecent Proposition

An Indecent Affair

An Indecent Arrangement

An Indecent Longing

An Indecent Desire

SALON GAMES
Invite Me In

Reserve My Nights

Expose My Desire

Keep My Secrets

Rock My Heart

LOVERS UNDERCOVER

Lovers & Lies

Sinners & Secrets

Beauty & Brains

Thieves & Thrills

FORGOTTEN GODDESSES

What A Goddess Wants

How to Worship A Goddess

Goddess in the Middle

Where A Goddess Belongs

DARKLY ENCHANTED

Spell Bound

Moon Bound